A
John Quinton Cord
Novel

Lyon's Claw

Betty J. Vaughn

TotalRecall Publications, Inc.
1103 Middlecreek
Friendswood, Texas 77546
281-992-3131 TEL
www.totalrecallpress.com

All rights reserved. Except as permitted under the United States Copyright Act of 1976, No part of this publication may be reproduced, stored in a retrieval system, or transmitted in any form or by any means electronic or mechanical or by photocopying, recording, or otherwise without prior permission of the publisher. Exclusive worldwide content publication / distribution by TotalRecall Publications, Inc.

Copyright © 2020 by: Betty J. Vaughn
All rights reserved

ISBN: 978-1-59095-559-8
UPC: 6-43977-45595-6

Printed in the United States of America with simultaneous printings in Australia, Canada, and United Kingdom.

FIRST EDITION
1 2 3 4 5 6 7 8 9 10

This is a work of fiction. The characters, names, events, views, and subject matter of this book are either the author's imagination or are used fictitiously. Any similarity or resemblance to any real people, real situations or actual events is purely coincidental and not intended to portray any person, place, or event in a false, disparaging or negative light.

The scanning, uploading and distribution of this book via the Internet or via any other means without the permission of the publisher is illegal and punishable by law. Please purchase only authorized electronic editions, and do not participate in or encourage electronic piracy of copyrighted materials. Your support of the author's rights is appreciated.

To
Judy C. Gordon, Ed.D

With gratitude for a lifetime of friendship, and her invaluable help in bringing this book to fruition.

About the Author

Betty J. Vaughn has written all of her life, winning awards in school and afterwards. Following a career teaching AP art history and painting, she wrote her first novel, Yesterday's Magnolia, quickly followed by four historical novels. The Man in the Chimney; Turbulent Waters; Run, Cissy, Run, and The Intrepid Miss LaRoque. The four novels in the historical series were all winners of the award for historical fiction from the NC Society of Historians. The latest novel, Tiger's Code, deals with concerns that currently plague our Nation as well as many others. A graduate of East Carolina University and a prize winning watercolorist, Mrs. Vaughn is a resident of Raleigh, NC, enjoys traveling, gardening, gourmet cooking, and reading. She is currently researching for her next book.

"Mrs. Vaughn can consider herself a seasoned novelist. Her books are fast paced, action packed, and full of adventure. Her work isn't just a flurry of words, dry and boring. She is a master of literary technique as she weaves together a tapestry of words."

Editor's comments

Betty J. Vaughn's book, *Lyon's Claw*, the third book in the Quint Cord series, transports readers through settings and scenes so artistically crafted that they vicariously experience French and Swiss landscapes while viewing them through the kaleidoscopic lens of the characters. It is apparent in the opening pages that Quint Cord, former CIA operative and his newlywed wife, Lila, a former hacker, are on tenuous ground as they struggle to achieve normalcy in their lives.

As the storyline progresses, the reader experiences one suspenseful episode after another as Quint and several CIA operatives embark on various schemes to save his kidnapped wife, Lila, from self-serving thugs. The book explores the use of modern weaponry and remotely controlled aircraft in covert missions which is both timely and pertinent to potential US government operations on the today's world stage.

Lyon's Claw leads the reader on a captivating, exciting adventure. The fast-paced, intricately developed plot is spellbinding from beginning to end. This is another thriller by a master storyteller.

Judy C. Gordon, Ed.D.

Chapter 1

Quint Cord and his wife, the new Mrs. Lila Carson Cord, lay on the shingle beach in the small cove of Le Bestouan, which was but a short distance from Cassis. Both were content and tired from a night of celebration following the flight from Raleigh to Paris and then to the airport in Marseilles where they rented a car before driving to the small village. Cassis lay just to the east of the spectacular fjords called calanques in the local dialect. The aroma of maquis and sea made every breath a sensory delight. Sparkling in the dazzling sun, their skin was covered with glistening plankton from the sea. Not even the rocks beneath their blanket disturbed them as the song of cicadas lulled them into sleep. After a nap, both awakened ready for another dip in the sea before returning to their luxurious suite in the Hotel Les Roches Blanches and dressing for dinner.

Lila groaned as she laboriously navigated the pebble strewn shore to the water trying to protect tender feet, while Quint laughed at her antics as he followed her in. Both maneuvered to stand over one of the warm thermal springs that vented from the sea in the small cove. The warm water from the vents bubbled up into the Mediterranean which was still cold from winter melt making for an instant contrast between warm and cold.

Lila lifted her face to the sun and closed her eyes. "I love it here, Quint. How did you know about Cassis? It is a little off the beaten track for most Americans, I suspect."

"My parents brought me here years ago. I've loved it ever since." He went on to describe the things that drew him to the south of France. Mesmerized, Lila listened as he described a Provence that continued to call to him. He explained how the Camargue lies at the mouth of the Rhone river.

There miles of wind-swept, sun-drenched marshlands drowse beneath azure skies flecked with raucously wheeling sea birds. Wild horses once roamed the grassy plans unfettered by man. Now they were herded by Gitanos, the Camargue gypsies. Dotted about the Camargue were white-washed houses with the northeastern ends rounded to withstand the powerful Mistral wind which comes howling out of the Alps. In easy proximity to the marshes are Nimes, Arles, St. Remy-de-Provençe with its ancient Roman ruins, Les Baux with its roguish past and romantic present, and the papal palace in Avignon. The towns of Aix-en-Provençe and Cezanne's home Le Mistral, Marseille with its picturesque Vieux Port, and the Crusader port of Aigues Mortes which basks within thick stone walls are but a short drive from Cassis. Fjords of crystal-clear water slit the Mediterranean coast between Marseille and Cassis with rugged grandeur. Cites and countryside, Alpilles hills and marshy plains, all washed by the brilliant Provençal sunlight, has been a lure to artists since the Impressionist period.

Lila exclaimed, "What an image you paint with words. You make me want to see all of this area…all of the places you have described."

"Your wish is my command." Quint smiled and pointed, "My dad loved the movie The French Connection. See that white house on the cliff there to your right, part of the movie was filmed there."

"You know, I don't think I ever saw that movie." Lila studied the house that stood beneath maritime pines. The dark trunks and vibrant green foliage provided dramatic contrast to the stark white of the house against the turquoise blue of the sky. A slight breeze made shadows ripple on the walls of the structure. "Wow, what a beautiful place to have a home. If we lived there, I would never want to leave."

"Hey, if you want it, I'll see if I can buy it." Quint grinned, only half joking.

"Really! You never did tell me, but just how rich are you."

"Very… and now it's how rich *we are*."

"I can dig that. Boy, just an 'I do' and I went from poor working girl to a rich lady of leisure."

"Are you going to miss working as a hacker for the CIA? I don't want you to get bored, but I am so glad we resigned, even if Gerald is determined to get us back." Gerald Williams, Director of the CIA, was beyond upset when Quint turned in their resignations right after the last job which had almost seen Lila killed. As it was, she had spent weeks in a coma, before making a slow recovery.

"Judging by the itinerary you have for our honeymoon it's going to be awhile before we are home long enough to even think about work. Besides, after all the romancing on this trip, I may have a growing tummy by the time we return."

"I am doing my darned level best, darling." Quint grinned down at her. "What say we go on back to the hotel and take a little nap before dressing for dinner?"

"Nap, my eye! I'm on to you, lover boy. Not that I mind, but do you think we could leave a little early and walk along the quay before dinner? La Nono D'Oro is on the quay, I think."

"It is and we can. But that just means you are going to be up late again tonight, Mrs. Cord." Quint lifted his eyebrows in a lecherous wiggle.

"I'll try to stay awake," Lila teased.

"Are you sure you don't want to go back to La Villa Madie tonight instead of trying La Nona D'Oro? That was a fabulous meal last night. Madie is worth every one of those Micheline stars."

"Maybe we can go back tomorrow night, Quint. Tonight, I want to check out Port St. Pierre and see if we can book a tour of the calanques tomorrow. They sound gorgeous from the write-up in the tour guide in the hotel."

"They are stunning, and I was definitely going to book us for a tour. We'll have the hotel pack a picnic lunch for the captain and us. We'll do the private tour and make a day of it."

An hour later they were ambling along the quay looking at the various watercraft harbored in the small port. The huge red cliffs of Cap Canaille loomed over the east end of the port. Quint nodded toward it and commented, "It means Cape of Thieves in English. This area was a haven for smugglers and pirates at one time."

"Well, let's hope they've all left."

Attracted by a pretty little boutique, Lila said, "Do you mind if I duck in this shop? I just saw a sundress that I would love to have. It's perfect for the weather here and will be great on Figure Eight, too."

"Sure. I think I'll walk down to the newsstand and pick up a copy of USA Today. Would you like a magazine or something?"

"No thanks, you don't leave me any time for much reading." Lila laughed as she walked into the shop.

The man behind the counter looked up and smiled at the pretty American. "Bonjour, Madame."

"Bonjour!" Lila was aware he was studying her as she

thumbed through the rack until she found another like the dress displayed in the window. Turning up the tag, she saw it was in her size. She walked over to the mirror on the wall in back and held the dress up to her body. She smiled at her reflection, pleased with the way her long blond hair, pulled back and held off her face, enhanced the green of her eyes. The vibrant emerald green dress was going to be a hit with Quint. It was sexy without being overtly so. She could already picture it on her trim, curvaceous body.

"Would you like to try the dress, Madame? There is a dressing closet just behind you."

"No, Merci. This looks perfect. I loved it the minute I saw it in the window."

"Ah, bon." The man rang up the sale and wrapped the dress in tissue before carefully placing it in a bag. Again, he studied her face. "Many pardons, Madame, but your face looks familiar. Are you a star in the cinema, or some other celebrity?"

"You flatter me! I am no one of any fame, trust me. My husband and I are here on our honeymoon."

"You must congratulate him for me. You are a beautiful woman…une belle femme."

"Thank you." Lila took the bag he handed her and left the shop to find Quint waiting outside reading the front page of the newspaper.

"Hey, what are you frowning and looking so serious about?" Lila pecked him on the cheek. When he turned the paper so she could read the headline, Lila gasped. "Good grief! How on earth does anyone know about me? I thought Gerald said my role in bringing down that Chinese maniac would never see the light of day."

"Obviously someone at the agency leaked. If I knew who, I'd take him behind the shed and beat him senseless. Doesn't the idiot know this could be dangerous for you?"

Lila studied her photo in the center of the front page alongside that of Chen Dai, the Chinese hacker who had planted a virus inside North Korean, U.S., and Chinese GPS satellites around the China Sea allowing him to crash navigation systems throughout the area. He was responsible for several shipwrecks, plane crashes, and North Korean missile detonations that destroyed a Japanese village and took out half of the U.S. base at Futenma, Japan. Lila had been instrumental in tracking and identifying him for the CIA. Discovering that she was after him, he tried to stop her by causing a near fatal car wreck. When she survived that, he had tracked her to Quint's home on Figure Eight Island on the coast of North Carolina. Only Quint's timely arrival had saved her and resulted in the arrest of Chen. After his arrest, both the CIA and FBI had subjected him to rigorous questioning prior to turning him over to the Chinese for extradition and a trial in China. It was all neatly laid out in the article.

Quint tapped the paper. "It's front page here, also The Herald Tribune, and French papers that are in the rack over there."

"You know, the shopkeeper just told me I look like someone famous. I shrugged it off and told him I'm just a nobody here on my honeymoon. You don't think this is a problem, do you?"

"I don't know, but I'm not happy to have these papers proclaiming you the most talented hacker on the planet. I don't like the world knowing where we live, either. There are some bad dudes out there that would love to use someone with your talent to create all kinds of chaos. I'm going to call Gerald and see how this happened. I suspect he will be as pissed as I am."

Gerald Williams, the Director of the CIA, had assigned both Quint and Lila to the Chen case.

"Can we just check out the tour boats and have dinner? I'd like to try to forget about that darned article and not let it ruin our time here." Lila's eyes pleaded with him as he stood lost in thought.

Finally, he shrugged. "Yeah, I don't want this to spoil our honeymoon either. Maybe I'm just over-reacting."

They continued walking down the quay, looking at the boats anchored in the harbor and commenting on their names and home ports. For Quint, who was lost in thought, the luster was off the evening despite Lila's attempts to cheer him up. They booked a ticket for the next day with a charming captain before returning to La Nona D'oro for dinner.

As they walked to their table, Quint's phone dinged to let him know he had a text message. Walking behind Lila, he extracted the phone from his pocket and read the message. It was from Gerald, who was as irate as he. The leaker was a file clerk who read the classified folder on the Chen affair without proper authorization and told her boyfriend, an aspiring reporter for the Washington Post. From there the story went viral. The clerk was fired but there was no retracting the story. Gerald suggested they curtail the honeymoon and come to Washington where they would be placed under the witness protection program. That suggestion was not an option for him, and he knew without asking, that Lila would reject it out of hand. Neither of them wanted to live like prisoners with aliases in some locale of government choosing. He regretted his decision to ever work for the CIA and to allow Lila to become a part of the agency. Unknowingly both of their lives were forever compromised.

When they were seated at the table, Lila asked, "Anyone important messaging you?"

"No. It was just Buster congratulating us and wishing us all the best. Nothing to worry about." Quint did not meet her eyes as he studiously perused the menu. Even so, he suspected Lila saw through the lie. She was intuitive that way. Thankfully, she chose not to pursue it, allowing the subject to drop as she, too, studied the menu.

"I'm no good at French, babe. What is this Brandade de Morue stuff?"

"That's a local dish made with cod that is pounded in cream, olive oil, truffles, and garlic. It's pretty rich."

"Oh, that's not for me. What are you having?"

Quint tapped his selection on her menu, "I love bourride. It's a fish soup served with croutons and aioli. That and a salade vert are perfect for me."

"Salade vert, green salad," she guessed. "Soup and a salad sound great. I'll have the same thing."

Quint ordered the meal along with a nice bottle of white Rhone wine. When the meal came, he made an effort to participate in her chatter about the area. Having never been out of the States, Lila was like a child under the Christmas tree. Each new thing was exciting and something to be talked about. He listened half-heartedly and managed to make the needed responses. But something kept tickling the back of his mind.

Suddenly he blurted, "Lila, would you mind if I changed the itinerary? There is a small little town in Tuscany I think you would love."

"Italy! I would love it. When do we leave?" she squealed. "Wait, does that mean we aren't going to Paris?"

"I'm not sure, Lila. This article in the paper has me worried. For the moment, I suspect we will be wiser to go somewhere a bit off the beaten track."

"So, does that mean the boat trip is off, too?"

"No, no. We will do the boat tour tomorrow and leave in a couple of days, I think. I'll need to make some arrangements first. I'll start that first thing tomorrow. We don't need to be at the boat until 10:30 so that should give me time to make some calls."

He did not tell her that the day before leaving for Italy; he would be going to Paris alone. He needed to visit the long-term locker he rented in the Charles de Gaulle airport. In the locker, were alternate passports, materials for disguises that would alter his appearance to match the photo in the desired passport, two handguns with ammunition, and extra untraceable cell phones with charging cords. He had another locker in London equipped in a similar manner, and yet another in Rome. He had considered going to the one in Rome, but the CIA agency in Paris had an excellent staff on hand for what he needed for Lila. She would no longer be traveling under her own name. While he was away for the day, he would arrange for her to spend her time at a local spa. Shorter hair and a dye job would help to alter her appearance. Gerald would have a photo of Lila emailed to the Paris office where his men would change the image to suit her new identity. When they left for the villa in Tuscany…one that he had used before…they would be traveling as Mr. Leonard White, an investment banker from Charlotte, N.C., and his wife Carolyn. He had other passports, but the Leonard one was the best disguise. With graying temples, glasses, a generic but well-tailored business suit, and a little padding around the middle he looked nothing like himself. Quint had the kind of look that was perfect for his role with the CIA. He was neither tall nor short, not fat nor skinny; and he was nice looking without being strikingly handsome. His ability to blend in and readily assume another identity was an asset in his former job as an operative. Lila was more striking. There was nothing he could do about that beyond her hair and some large sunglasses. Perhaps, while they were staying in Tuscany, he would think of something else to help her avoid detection.

Aware that Lila had said something; he looked up, "Huh?"

Lila made a small moue, "I said, do you like your meal?"

"I'm sorry, Lila. I was just figuring out the Italian trip, so I didn't hear you."

"What can I do to help?"

"For now, nothing. Just enjoy your time here. I'm sorry about the change of plans, but it's best for the moment. I must make a quick trip to pick up some things we are going to need. I also will be turning in this car and renting another."

"Can I go with you wherever it is you're going?"

"I won't be gone long, and I can do what I need to do better by myself. Besides, I want you to enjoy your last day here so I'm booking you into a spa." Before she could protest, he continued, "Lila, you need a change of looks so you are not so recognizable. We both do. While you are at the spa, I want you to have your hair changed into a short, brunette bob with bangs that sweep down on the sides to help hide your face."

"I don't want chopped-off black hair!"

"It won't be forever. You can always grow it back."

Lila turned and stared out at the dark water of the harbor where the lights of the restaurants lining the quay danced in merry reflection. She pouted for several minutes while Quint waited her out. Turning back to him, she demanded, "Do you know how long it will take my hair to grow back out to the length it is now? Why can't I just wear a wig?"

"If I thought that would be as safe, you could; however, I don't think that. Please, you will still be my beautiful wife. It won't be forever."

"No? How long?"

"Babe, I wish I knew. I'm going to trust my gut on this and it's telling me we need to lay low."

"Geez, Quinton Cord, you are turning into a bossy husband."

Nudging her foot under the table, Quint smiled softly. "Hey, lady, I'm a husband that's madly in love with his wife...and wants her safe."

In her little girl voice, Lila murmured, "I love you, too. Dammit, I hate this! I'd like to wring the neck of the stupid twit that leaked our identities."

With a heart-felt sigh, Quint responded, "So would I!"

Frustration held them in its thrall for the remainder of the evening. Although the boat trip to the calanques was an exhilarating one for Lila, and the picnic a success, Quint had a difficult time relaxing. Knowing he was worried, Lila tried not to bug him about it. The following day, he left at sunrise to drive to the airport for the flight to Paris. Lila was restless after he left and unable to go back to sleep. Her appointment for the spa and a hair make-over wasn't until 11:00. By 7:00 she had completed her room service breakfast, dressed in the new frock she had purchased on the quay, and was ready for a stroll on the beach.

Lila donned thick soled shoes to make the shingled beach less difficult to navigate. In three minutes, she reached the deserted Bestouan and began a brisk walk along the edge of the water.

Lila wondered where Quint had gone. She could only hope that all the precautions, that he thought necessary, were unneeded. The thought of living under an assumed name and constantly looking over one's shoulder had no appeal as a way of life. She wondered when they would be able to return to Quint's home on Figure Eight; and if they did, would they need twenty-four-hour guards to keep them safe. Lila's life had changed dramatically when Quint had indirectly recruited her for the CIA. If only he had not told Gerald Williams about her skills in hacking, she would still be a professor of computer science at North Carolina State University in Raleigh. Quint had a house in Raleigh, as well as the one on the coast. They could have spent more time in Raleigh and gone on with their lives.

She smiled when she thought of her husband. Theirs had been an on-again, off-again relationship as Quint was determined to keep an emotional distance because of the danger of his work with the CIA. In the end, he had fallen in love despite himself. That was long after she realized she was in love with him. He made her happy, and he certainly was bringing her a much more exciting life with the money to travel and have luxuries she had only dreamed of as a single working woman. The fact that he was wealthy had not factored into her falling for him. She had dated men with money before…men that were better looking, more romantic, and far more available. But, something about Quint kept drawing her back. There was a genuineness, a basic goodness about Quint that made him reliable, someone she could always depend on to be there for her. It didn't hurt that the chemistry between them was off the charts.

Lila heard steps behind her but ignored them. As the sound drew nearer, she glanced over her shoulder. Remembering

Quint's warning to be careful, she began to walk faster. If she hurried, she could reach the quay in minutes. There people would be going to work in restaurants and shops in order to prepare for opening.

Chapter 2

The desk clerk at the Hotel Les Roches Blanches glanced up when the man entered the lobby. The middle-aged businessman did not look like any guest that he had checked in, but perhaps the gentleman had registered when he was not on duty. He shrugged his shoulders as the man walked past and went back to working the crossword puzzle that he kept on the counter to pass the time when things were idle.

With his identity so remarkably changed, Quint did not dare stop at the desk for a key. He hoped Lila was in the room and her phone was on silent as she was not answering his calls. The moment he landed at the airport in Marseilles he had called to let her know he was back, and he called again when he was in his newly rented car and driving back to Cassis. Quint was not unduly worried, as she had assured him, she would stay in the hotel while he was away. He glanced towards the pool as he walked through the lobby but did not see her there. Walking down the hall to their room, he whistled softly under his breath. He was relieved that he had obtained new identity papers, a different car, and an untraceable phone. Gerald Williams had called the Rome office to arrange a rented villa near Siena paid for with an untraceable card. Once in the room, he would call the front desk and have the charges put on his old credit card. Hopefully, Lila would have packed their bags and be ready to leave. After that, he prayed no one could track them to the new location.

When he reached their door, he knocked softly and called,

"Lila, it's me. Let me in, babe."

He waited for a minute but there was no response. Leaning his head against the door, he listened to see if he could hear her moving within. No sound emerged from the silent room. He knocked again more loudly, but again she did not open the door. Quint shifted from foot to foot wondering what to do. He could not go to the front desk in disguise. He would have to return to his own appearance until he could track his wife down. Turning back towards the lobby, he entered the restroom near the pool entrance. Pulling the padding from under his shirt, he rolled it up and put it inside his briefcase with his new identity documents and weapon. He then used a wet towel to wipe the gray color from his hair and eyebrows. It would not be a problem to recolor his hair with the spray container in the side compartment of his briefcase. Finally, he removed the horn-rimmed glasses and studied himself in the mirror. He looked nothing like the man that had returned to the hotel moments earlier.

Quint returned to the lobby and walked up to the receptionist. The man looked up and smiled, "Ah, Mr. Cord, what may I do for you?"

"I see you still have our room key in your box. Do you know if my wife is in the hotel somewhere?"

The man thought for a minute, "I'm trying to remember. I don't think I have seen her since early this morning when I began my shift. That would have been around 7:30. She said she was going for a walk along the beach. She has not been back to the room since. I would know if she had returned for the key and then left again."

Quint's face slowly drained of color. Forcing himself not to panic, he asked, Do you know if anyone came here asking for us?"

"No. You have had no visitors."

"I see. Thank you. May I have the room key?"

"Bien sur, monsieur. I am sure your wife will be back soon. Is there anything more I may do for you?"

"No, no. That's all for now."

It was a frightened man that dashed down the hall. When he reached their door, he opened it and walked in calling for his wife. When there was no answer Quint quickly checked the bedroom and bath. All looked much as it had when he left that morning except for the remade bed and fresh towels, where room service had cleaned the suite. Their toiletries and clothes were still in the same places. Their luggage had not been packed. He checked Lila's things in the closet and saw that her new green dress was missing, so she must have been wearing that when she left the suite. Her purse and phone were gone. Apparently, she had taken those with her when she left to walk. Once again, he dialed her number, praying she would answer. Her phone immediately went to the answering machine. "Lila, it's Quint. Where are you, babe? Give me a call; you have me worried. I love you."

Quint paced the floor for the next hour while the room slowly grew dark as the sun sank below the horizon. Glancing at his watch he saw that it was after 7:00. She had now been gone nearly twelve hours. Something was badly wrong, or she would be here. He stared at the dial on his phone before punching in Gerald's number.

"Gerald, there's a problem here. Lila's gone missing. As best as I can tell, she left to go for a walk about twelve hours ago and no one has seen her since."

The CIA director tried to keep his voice flat, but Quint could sense the man's unease when he responded, "Would you like me to send an agent to help you search?"

Quint hesitated before answering, "You know, if Buster Walton is back from vacation, I'd like him here. Right now, I want someone that has my back. Even if Lila walks through the door in the next five minutes, another man is just added security. I flat out don't feel good about her being gone. She knew we were planning to leave the minute I got back and was supposed to have our bags packed and be ready to go. She is not irresponsible, dammit! Even though she was not as worried about this mess as I am, she agreed that we need to lay low for a while." Buster the former SEAL who ran his own agency as a contractor to the CIA, had worked with Quint on a couple of previous jobs. The man had an oversized personality and a tendency to flirt with anything in skirts, but when the chips were down, he was the toughest guy around.

"Sure, I'll call him and get him there on the next plane smoking. He considers you a friend, so even if he's still on vacation, he'll be there for you guys. I don't have to tell you how much I regret that damned article and the danger it put you in. I particularly hate it for Lila since the last job nearly got her killed. Hopefully, she decided to spend the day out and just isn't back yet. By the way, I didn't tell you, but the President is closely following her file. We both feel she could be an asset in creating new hack-proof security devices."

"I'm hoping she's finished with all of that. It's too dangerous. Do you think I enjoy wondering every moment whether her life is in danger? Mine I can handle, but not hers! Hell, man, for all we know she's been kidnapped by some evil people for who knows what reason. At some point, enough is enough. Right now, the only thing I want to do is find her and take her somewhere she'll be safe. You owe us that."

"You're right, Quint. Just calm down. I'm going to do all I can to help you. You do what you can in the meantime while I work on things from this end."

"Thanks, Gerald. I don't mean to get in your face. It's just that I'm scared."

"I understand. You let me know if you learn anything. I'll get back to you soon."

Quint killed the call and paced around the room several times. He could not stay in the room and worry. He had to do something. He walked over to the desk and grabbed a pen and sheet of paper. When he had finished the note, he wrote her name on the envelope and propped it against the lamp which he left on. If she returned, she would know to wait until he came back.

He stopped at the front desk to drop off the key before beginning his walk along the shore of the cove towards the restaurants and lights of Quai Jean Jacques Barthélémy. As he walked, he asked anyone he met if they had seen a woman walking along the shore earlier. None had. In the restaurants, he queried the waiters and walked casually among the tables apologizing for interrupting and again asking if anyone had seen his wife. Returning to the quay he continued towards Port St. Pierre. He passed the shop where he remembered Lila buying the dress. She had commented that the owner seemed to recognize her. On an impulse, he turned back and entered the shop. The owner smiled in welcome.

Quint explained that his wife was missing since walking on the beach that morning and he wished to know if the man had seen her that day. He watched as the owner's face blanched and his eyes shifted towards the wall. Quint probed, "She said you seemed to recognize her. Perhaps, you saw her photo in the local paper and remembered her face. Is that so?"

Refusing to meet Quint's eyes, the man stammered his reply, "No, no, no…I flirt only. She is very beautiful."

"Yes, she is. Thank you for your time." He started towards the door before turning back for a parting shot, "By the way, the gendarmerie and the agents of my government may be coming by to question you in the next day or so."

"Oui?"

"Yes."

Quint left the shop and took a seat on a bench down the way where he had a clear view of the shop. In moments, the owner pulled in the merchandise on the exterior of the shop, then closed and shuttered his business. Five minutes after that, he turned the key in the door, locked it, and walked rapidly down the quay in the opposite direction. As he walked, he pulled his cell phone from his pocket and began talking in rapid French interspersed with the local dialect. Quint followed but was too far away to pick up more than occasional words. The only thing that registered was the high pitch of the man's voice. He was obviously unhappy.

Quint followed him to the parking lot where the man got in his car and drove off. The only thing Quint could do was read the license plate and identify the make of the car. There was no way he could follow on foot. Returning to the quay, he again walked along the port asking any he met if they had seen a woman earlier matching his wife's description. Feeling hopeless, he turned back to the hotel. The key was still in the slot at the concierge desk. He asked for it and returned to their suite. His note was where he had left it. Never had he felt so lonely or frightened as in that moment.

His stomach growled to remind him that he had taken no time to eat since the previous evening's dinner. Calling room-service he ordered a meal. When it came, he chewed methodically. Afterwards he could not have said what he had eaten. He removed his jacket and tie and stretched out on the bed. Although he was exhausted, there was no way he could sleep. Sometime after that, his phone pinged to let him know he had a message. Snatching it from the bedside table, he read, "Help me."

Frantically texted back, "Lila, where are you?"

He stared at the screen for the next hour praying for a response, but none came. He repeatedly tried calling, but there was no answer. Now he knew. Someone had taken his wife. She was alive but in trouble. His only choice was to find her and fast.

He stared out the window at the starlit sky, wondering where Lila was. Calling Gerald, he quickly informed him that Lila was in trouble and had texted him.

"Have you heard anymore since the text?" Gerald asked.

"Nothing. I texted her to let me know where she is, but there was no reply. I tried calling, but she still doesn't answer."

"Give me a few minutes and I will have our guys track her cell phone. Buster is on the way; and I also phoned my local assets in Marseilles to alert them to what is going on. They should be getting in touch shortly. They have a good handle on the local bad guys. If it's someone that's not local, we can scan EU entries for passports of any known perps. As you know, now it's more difficult to catch those who are citizens within the EU, since they don't need to show a passport to move from country to country. One way or another, we will find her. Try not to worry and get some rest. I'll call back with anything I learn."

"Thanks, Gerald. I'll do the same as soon as I know anything new."

At some point Quint had fallen into a restless sleep. The buzzing of the phone in his ear did not at first register. Groggily, he sat up and reached for the phone on the bedside table. "Yes?"

"My apologies for calling so early, Monsieur Cord. There is a gentleman here who says he is a friend of yours. His name is Monsieur Buster Walton."

"Thank you. Would you put him on the phone, please?"

"Of course." Quint heard the desk clerk speak to Buster. In a moment Buster was on the line.

"Hey, man. I know you aren't in the mood for small talk, so I'll make it fast. I have checked in here. As soon as I can get a shower, would you meet me downstairs for breakfast? We'll come up with a plan and see if we can get this thing rolling. What say we meet on the terrace in thirty? Is that good for you?"

"That's fine. And, thanks Buster. I hate to cut your vacation short, but Lila and I really need you on the team."

"That's what friends are for. Now get your butt in gear. It's time to get cracking, old buddy. We are going to find Lila."

Quint smiled at Buster's take charge attitude. Unlike Quint who was more introspective and deliberate, he was one for jumping in with both feet. It made them a good team. He walked into the lobby 25 minutes later and snagged a local paper from the stand near the front desk. He began thumbing through as he waited for Buster to come down from his room. A photo on the inside page caught his eye. The man looked familiar, but for the moment he could not put a name with the face. Buster walked up as he stood there staring at the picture. He tucked the paper under his arm. He would get back to it later.

Buster patted him on the shoulder, "Hey, Buddy. I sure am sorry about Lila. This purely sucks."

Quint twisted his mouth into a wry grin, "Yeah, it certainly spoiled our honeymoon."

"Let's hope it won't be long before you have her back." As they walked to a table on the terrace, Buster commented, "Boy, you know how to pick'em. This place is first class. And look at that view."

Both men sat at the table. When the waitress bustled up, they gave their order and leaned back in their chairs, momentarily lost in thought.

Suddenly, Quint sat up. Unfolding his newspaper, he opened it to the photo and began to read. After several minutes, he looked at Buster and declared, "Dammit, look at this. Can you read French?"

"Some, but I'm slow. Tell me what it's about."

Quint stabbed his finger at the man in the photo. "He's the one. I knew I recognized his face."

Buster interrupted, "You lost me. What are you talking about?"

Quint explained about Lila going into a shop to buy a dress and the owner of the boutique recognizing her and asking her if she were famous. He then explained how he had walked along the quay the night before asking people if they had seen his wife. Remembering the shop, he said he had walked in to question the owner. "He seemed a little shifty at the time, not quite meeting my eyes. Not long after I left the shop, he closed and left. I tracked him as far as his car, but since I was on foot I couldn't tell where he was going."

Quint stared at the face in the paper before continuing, "According to this, Rene Gaston was murdered last night not long after he closed his business for the day. This says he was a long-time shop owner here in Cassis with no known enemies. It remarks that despite a recent and costly divorce, there is no reason to suspect suicide or his ex-wife's involvement. It doesn't say where he was found or how he was murdered."

Buster moved the notepad he had brought with him to the table to his right side. Taking a pen from his pocket, he looked up at Quint. "Let's make a list of things to do. Then we can prioritize and assign each item."

"Good idea. Number one is to get Gerald's guy in Marseilles nosing into this murder and see what the Cassis police have. Number two is to see if Gerald has located Lila's phone so we know where to begin looking for her. Number three... I'm drawing a blank. You got any suggestions?"

"I say we go down to the quay and get friendly with the local shop owners. They don't know me, and they probably won't remember you. I figure we act like two dumb and curious tourists. Be friendly, see if one or two will join us for a drink. They may know something the newspaper reporter didn't. At least it's a place to start."

Quint agreed, "That's a plan then. Let's finish breakfast; then I want to run back to the room for a minute. How about texting Gerald and give him this new info while I'm gone. It's the middle of the night in Washington, so he will be a while getting back to us, I suspect."

Fifteen minutes later, trying to look as much like tourists as possible, they left the hotel headed for the quay.

Chapter 3

Lila groaned as she awakened from a drug induced stupor. Her body was cramped, her eyes were blindfolded, and her hands and feet were tied. She vaguely remembered coming to at some point and working her phone from her pocket. Using one finger she began texting Quint to help her, but before she could type more, she heard the door open. Frantically she tapped send and tried to hide the phone from her captor. Seeing what she was attempting, he snatched it from her. Another hypodermic had sent her back to la-la land. Biting back another groan so he would not be aware that she was awake, she tried to remember what had happened. The last she remembered was the man following her on the beach had come up to her and forced her to go with him. When they reached his car, he had unlocked the trunk and shoved her in. She remembered being given a shot and then everything went black.

She nudged her feet over to her right and felt a low railing; when she moved to her left, she encountered what seemed to be a wall. The rocking of her bed and the thrum of a powerful motor suggested she was in a boat. She had no idea where she was being taken nor who had seized her. She lay still trying to determine what to do to save herself, to escape, or to stall whatever they had planned for her until Quint could find her.

She could lie still no longer. It felt as though her kidneys would burst. If she did not go to the toilet soon, she would further lose any dignity left to her. She hated to alert the man that she was awake, but she had no choice.

Lila called, "Can anyone hear me? I need to go to the bathroom, please."

From somewhere, she could hear murmuring before the door burst open and her captor snarled, "What is it?"

"I need to use the bathroom. Please let me up. If you undo my hands and feet, I promise not to try to get away.

The man's laugh was harsh, "Lady, I'm not worried about you getting away. You may not have noticed, but we are at sea."

"Please, undo me and show me to the bathroom. I beg you."

"Do nothing to upset me, or you will regret it. Do you understand?"

"Yes."

The man undid the ties binding her hands and feet but left the blindfold on. She did not remind him that she had seen his face if he was the man on the beach that had taken her. It did not occur to her that the man she was talking to may not have been the one that had forced her to go with him. Grabbing her by the arm, he snatched her to her feet and shoved her before him. Lila tripped but caught herself against a door jamb.

"It's on your right. Keep the blindfold on. If you untie it, I will know. You do not want to piss me off. For two cents, I would throw you to the sharks and be done with you."

"I'll do my best not to annoy you," she responded with sarcasm. Lila heard him harrumph as she felt her way to the door of the head and opened it. Closing it behind her, she leaned back and took a deep breath to stop shaking. Fumbling with numbed hands, she was able to get her panties down and then find the toilet. Once done, she pulled her underwear up and felt for the sink. She washed her hands and wiped water on the lower part of her face and her neck. The cold water felt wonderful and for a moment she toyed with the idea of lifting the blindfold and bathing her eyes as well. Biting her lip as she remembered his words, she decided that would not be wise. She felt her way to the door and opened it. The man was waiting.

Lila forced a smile, before saying, "Thank you. I'm thirsty, too. May I have some water and food, please. I've had nothing since you took me."

He seized her by her arm and turned right leading her away from the cabin where she had been sleeping.

He commanded, "Step up."

She did as he asked, wondering where he was taking her. She feared, as he forced her forward, that she was about to be some shark's meal, rather than having something to assuage her own hunger and thirst. She thought about falling into a faint so if he planned to toss her into the sea, he would at least have to carry her there. Why should she help him kill her, she asked herself? Before she could make up her mind, he spoke.

"Sit down. You'll have something to eat and drink in a minute."

Lila nodded her thanks as she sat as directed. She heard the man climbing steps leading up from the galley and speaking to someone topside. The engine was loud enough that she could not discern what was being said. Lila shivered. The galley was cooler than the cabin due to a breeze coming from the portholes above her head. Huddling lower in her seat, she wrapped her arms around herself. If only she knew where they were taking her, she might be able to devise a way to save herself. Lila had never been so terrified. Her previous career as a college professor had done nothing to prepare her for the situation in which she now found herself. She could only surmise that she had been kidnapped because of the article in the paper. If that were the case, they would not want her dead despite the man's threat to throw her to the sharks. In that thought lay a certain amount of peace. If they wanted her expertise on a computer, she possibly would have a means of finding a way to get a message to Quint and the CIA. With the resources at their disposal, they would find her.

Lila thought about what she knew about the man holding her captive. It was precious little. She could not determine if he were the one who had taken her, or if she had been passed off to someone else. Thinking about the weight of his footsteps and what little she could deduce of his height as he had led her to the head and the galley, she suspected this was a second man... heavier and shorter than the man on the beach. He appeared to be a heavy smoker judging by the rasp in his voice. The man spoke with an accent, despite being fluent in English. She had not yet determined the type of accent. She didn't think it was French, but until she heard him talk more she could not say for sure.

The man descended into the galley followed by a second person. The second man, judging by his tread, appeared to not weigh as much. She remembered reading somewhere that victims should try to establish a personal relationship with their captors in order to make it more difficult for them to harm the victim. Trying to humanize herself and appeal to their better natures, she smiled in their direction and commented, "I don't know much about boats, but this sounds like a very powerful one. Are their many cabins? Do you own this? If so, how fortunate you are."

The younger man answered before the one she mentally

named Smoky could interfere, "No, we work for the owner. If I owned a boat like this, I wouldn't be doing what I do now."

Picking up on the troubled note in his voice, she said, "In that case, I hope the day will come when you will have your own boat."

Smoky commanded, "Enough chatter, you need to get some food cooking."

"Pronto. Why don't you open that bottle of wine on the shelf behind you? I could use a glass while I cook." The one ordered to cook directed a question to Lila, "Signora, would you like a glass of wine?"

"I am very thirsty. I would like water first and then some wine would be nice. Thank you for thinking of me."

Smoky growled, "You would think we are running a boarding house to listen to you two. Why don't you just do your job and shut up."

"There is no reason to make this any worse than it already is. The lady is behaving herself, so why can't we?"

Smoky growled but did not answer. She heard liquid being poured into a glass and then he sat it in front of her. "Water."

She grabbed the glass and quickly drained it. While she was drinking Smoky had opened the wine bottle and poured glasses for each of them. He sat hers in front of her. Lila reached for it cautiously to prevent bumping it over. The blindfold was a nuisance, but she did not try to lift it. If later, she was able to recognize them, her situation would become substantially more dangerous. The wine was excellent. She smiled with pleasure as she sipped it. She could feel her body relaxing and becoming more alert to subtle nuances. Somehow, the inability to see forced her to tune into her other senses. She could smell the aroma of onions, tomatoes, and garlic sizzling in hot oil. Her stomach growled in anticipation. She felt the texture of the seat to discover it was made of a buttery leather. The table where she sat was epoxied to the smoothness of silk. She heard another pot go on the stove and guessed the younger man was preparing to boil the pasta. Soon she could hear the little bubbles that rose to the surface of the heating water. He seemed to be chopping something. She hoped it was a salad and perhaps fresh basil for the pasta. Although she was no connoisseur of wines, she suspected the one she was sipping was an excellent Chianti. The meal, the wine, and the fact that he had called her signora, made her wonder if the younger man might be Italian. How ironic, she mused, if she should end up in Italy without Quint.

Neither man said anything more while the meal was being prepared. Lila was content to sit quietly trying to learn what she could about her situation. As she waited for their food, she could feel some of the fear and tension slipping away. Perhaps, once they had drunk enough wine, they would be more willing to talk to her. It was apparent that Smoky was the one in charge. Judging by his interaction with her since she had regained consciousness, she deemed him the meaner and more dangerous of the two. She would have to be careful not to anger him while trying to draw the younger man out. She decided to call him Chef for want of a name. She hoped the meal lived up to the title. She chuckled to herself; even if he couldn't cook, she was so hungry she would eat it anyway.

The rattle of dishes announced that the meal was being served. When they set the plate in front of her and ordered her to eat, she did not hesitate. Lila picked up her fork and using her left hand found her plate. She twirled some of the pasta around the fork and then paused. With a blindfold on, she could only hope to find her mouth and make the least possible mess. She did not want to stain the green dress she had bought, even though she suspected it was that very purchase at the boutique on the quay that had led to her kidnapping. Lila leaned well over her plate and began to eat. A few bites went astray despite her concentrated effort. Chef tucked a paper towel into her hand. Using it she kept her face as clean as she could.

"If you would let me remove the blindfold, I could eat this spaghetti a whole lot better you know."

She could hear the apology in his voice when Chef answered, "I'm sorry. We can't do that."

"Well, could you at least allow me to remove it when I am locked in the cabin. I promise I will tie it back on when you come to the door. Just knock before you unlock it. Please, I will lose some of my vision if you keep me for days on end with a blindfold on. I assume someone wants me to do some type of work on a computer. I can't, if my eyes are affected. I mean, if you don't want my computer expertise, why else would I have been taken?"

She heard the two men push back from the table and leave the galley. They climbed up to the deck. While it was impossible to make out words, it was obvious they were arguing. Hoping she had not made her situation worse, she could only sit and pray. After several minutes, they returned to the table.

Smoky snarled, "Alright. When we lock you in, you can take off the blindfold. But if you don't have it on when we open the damned door, I'm going to throw your ass overboard and I damned well mean it. Do you understand?"

"I do. I promise." Lila smiled and said, "Thank you."

Back in her cabin with her hands and feet untied and the blindfold removed, she hastened to look out the portholes to see if she could spot land and try to determine where they were headed. In every direction there was only water. In the distance, she could see a cruise ship, but it was too far away for her to try to signal. Spotting her shoulder bag in the corner, she hastily dug inside for her cell phone, but it was gone. Lila removed her dress and hung it from a cabinet knob. She then pulled the blanket from the bed and wrapped it around her to cover her body now clothed only in the lacy underwear she had bought for her honeymoon. She figured she had enough problems without tempting one of them to rape her. Although she thought Chef would probably not take advantage of her, she did not trust Smoky.

She looked around the cabin noting several lockers. She hoped one of them might hold something she could use to escape or to protect herself, if it should come to that. As quietly as she could, she eased each one open. In the first was a neatly folded tee shirt. She grabbed it and slipped it over her head. It came down to mid-thigh and gave her the modesty she needed. Continuing to churn through contents, it appeared there was nothing but clothes in the various lockers. She was ready to close the last one, when she felt something hard in a shirt pocket. Reaching in, she extracted a pocketknife. Lila quickly tucked it under the mattress on her berth. That done, she crawled in and wrapped herself in the blanket. As she settled into the berth, the light slowly faded from the sky. At least, with no blindfold and untied, she anticipated a less miserable night.

Even though she was far more comfortable, sleep was slow coming. For the first time in her life she was truly terrified. She was in the hands of strangers, bound for an unknown destination, and for a purpose she did not yet know. She thought of Quint and wondered where he was and what he was doing. She knew he would be searching for her, but had the man who had taken her left any clues he could use? She had no idea.

To keep from worrying about her predicament, Lila replayed their wedding in her mind. It had been under a rose covered arbor set up on the sandy beach in front of Quint's house on Figure Eight. His maid Teresa, loyal dog Code, and several friends had joined them in the celebration. Gerald Williams and his wife Jill were there, along with Buster, and a couple of her former colleagues from NC State University.

Afterwards they had eaten the feast Teresa had worked days to prepare...all washed down with a fine French champagne. She had helped Teresa decorate the house with sprays of roses and ready the guest house for the overnight guests. She felt a tear slip from the corner of her eye when she wondered if she would ever see their home again. Taking a deep breath, she forced the negative thoughts away. If she gave in to hopelessness, she would be unable to think clearly. The important thing was to be ready if the opportunity for escape presented itself. To do that, she had to be constantly alert and on the offensive. Rolling onto her side, she tried to go to sleep. The rock of the boat in the waves was lulling. After what must have been hours, she dozed in fitful sleep.

She was awakened by a knock on the door and the order to put the blindfold on. Lila quickly left the bed and put on her dress. Removing the knife from under the mattress, she slipped it in her bra. When that was done, she secured the blindfold and called out that she was ready. While she waited for the door to open, she slung her handbag over her shoulder. In it were her driver's license, credit cards, and some Euros. The key turned in the lock as she stood by the bunk wondering what was happening. The darkness beyond the windows had offered no clue despite a distant string of lights off the port side. Lila bit her lip and ordered herself to lift her chin and stop trembling. Whatever they planned, she was going to do her damnedest to escape. She could do nothing to help herself if she was paralyzed by fear.

The door swung open and Smoky ordered, "Out."

Stumbling forward, Lila felt for the door jamb. "What's going on? It's still night."

Chapter 4

Quint walked out of the bar where they had spent a fruitless hour talking to the bartender. It did not help that he had downed two glasses of Bordeaux while they sat at the bar. It was already midafternoon, and they had learned nothing more than what they knew when they started out after breakfast. He forced the fear to the back of his mind and turned left on the quay towards the harbor. Despite an hour with the police, another on the phone with Gerald, and hours talking with shopkeepers, bartenders, and waiters, they knew no more than they had known at breakfast. Quint looked over at Buster, his mouth twisted in concentration.

"I saw a camera on the lamppost back there. I wonder if it might have picked up something. There could be others around Cassis. Do you know if the police, checked them?"

"Remember, according to what the detective told us, they checked the cameras along the beach and in the parking lot. They saw her being put in the car. Apparently, they did not pick up on where the car was headed. I think they would have told us if they had."

"Let's talk to the port authority. I know it's an outside chance, but she could have been transferred to a boat. I thought about it and it seems to me that would be the least risky way of getting her out of here without being spotted."

"Yeah. It's worth a shot. Nothing else is turning up." Buster's voice reflected his own frustration after fruitless hours of searching for clues. Walking along the quay to the port authority's office, Buster slowed his steps every few feet. His enthusiastic exclamations of admiration for some of the boats was annoying to Quint who barely saw what he was passing. His total focus was on finding his wife.

Finally, he could take no more, "Step on it, Buster. You can admire the damned boats all you want once we find Lila."

Buster was instantly contrite, "I'm sorry. I'm an insensitive bastard. If I were in your shoes, I would be scared, frustrated, and totally pissed off."

"That about sums it up." Quint did not specify which part of the statement his comment addressed.

They walked the rest of the way to the port office and entered the door which was standing open. After explaining the purpose of their visit and showing their CIA credentials, the receptionist… wearing a name tag that identified her as Madame Marie Reynaud…asked them to sit. She disappeared through the door behind her desk. Several minutes later, she reappeared and asked them to follow her. As she led them down a hallway, Quint noticed Buster was again distracted. This time it was the shapely backside of the receptionist that held his admiring concentration. Quint shook his head. Buster was Buster. A friend, and a damned good man in his job; but now, he had no patience for him. He was just grateful he was there. Quint knew that Buster brought years of experience with the SEALS and then as a private contractor to the CIA. Quint's own expertise was in code cracking the old-fashioned analytical way. It was a skill that was fast becoming obsolete, as the world moved to computer technology and new kinds of encryption techniques. Lila was the expert there. Quint brought an insightful and inventive mind, carefully honed skills of self-protection and combat…that he had taught himself, and dogged determination once he was focused on something.

Buster glanced over at Quint and grinned. Shrugging his shoulders, he remarked, "This little town sure has some gorgeous scenery. I hope when this is over, I get to enjoy some of it."

Quint could not stop his chuckle, "God bless you, Buster. I hope it's soon."

Marie Reynaud paused at a door, this one with no window, and motioned to them to enter. Pointing them to chairs that faced three television screens corresponding to the three cameras the port authority used to surveil the premises, she said. "I have permission to share the films with you. Normally we have these for internal use and only share with the police in case of a crime on port property. However, since you are with the U.S. government, we are giving you permission to view them. If you find something that we need to report to the police, we ask you to share it with us. Could you tell me the time frame that you are interested in?"

Quint assured her that if they noticed anything that the police should be made aware of, they would point it out. He then gave her the dates and times that they wanted to see. "Also, there is a dress boutique on the quay called Jolie Madame. The owner was murdered yesterday..."

She interrupted, "Yes, I have shopped there many times. I was so sad to read of Rene's death in the paper this morning. He was always charming to me."

"Well, I'm decidedly not charmed. I have reason to believe he kidnapped my wife."

The woman's mouth formed a very large O. "Mon Dieu, I am so sorry Monsieur Cord." She said nothing more as she began typing commands into the computer to bring up the requested time frame on the three monitors. "I am going to set this to screen a faster replay than normal time. If you see something you need to study more closely, just interrupt me, and I can stop it or slow it down. Perhaps, I could help if I knew what you are looking for?"

Quint nodded, "Yes, that might be good. That way each of us has only one monitor to watch. I want to see whether Rene Gaston brought my wife to the port and put her on a boat before he was murdered. According to the hotel, she left to walk on the beach around 7:30. By the time shops opened, she was not seen, so the most critical time frame would be several hours of yesterday morning. If we see nothing during that period, we will continue to watch. I'm hoping something turns up as the police have no clues, and at this point, neither do we."

Marie smiled with empathy. "Ah, Monsieur Cord, I do hope that we find something to help you."

Buster gave her a wink and said, "Let's not be so formal. He's Quint and my name is Buster."

Marie nodded and repeated their names. "Call me Marie.

For the next hour and a half, they stared at the television screens. Outside Quint figured it was growing dark. His stomach growled to remind him he had eaten little. He hesitated to say anything for fear the woman would point out the time and say they would have to leave. After another thirty minutes, Buster began to fidget.

"Quint, if you can watch both my screen and yours, I'll go get us all something to eat from one of the cafes on the quay." Turning to Marie, he asked, "Does your husband expect you home at a certain time? We do not mean to inconvenience you, but we cannot afford to waste a minute trying to learn what happened to Lila."

"I am divorced. There is no husband, nor any children waiting for me. My boss expects me to remain until you are finished. There is always someone here, so we don't have to worry about staying."

Buster could not help the gleam in his eye as he looked at her with renewed interest. "His loss is our gain."

Marie shrugged in answer, but Quint could see a small smile that she struggled to quench.

"Would you like me to pick-up anything in particular, Quint? Marie?"

Never taking his eyes from the screen, Quint responded, "Anything. I don't care."

Marie replied, "Perhaps, it would be better if I go since you know what you are looking for and I don't."

Quint shook his head, "You say you knew Rene Gaston well, so you can more readily recognize the man than Buster who has never seen him…only the photo in the newspaper which wasn't very clear. Besides, we are unfamiliar with your equipment."

"Of course," she said. "You are correct."

Standing, Buster inquired, "What may I bring for you, Marie?"

"First, I will pause the replays, then I will write for you in French the name of the café. It is Le Perroquet. The owner knows me and what I like. He also will give you a better price if he knows I sent you. Give me a moment, and I will write it for you. The café is on the right just a short way down. It is easy to find. They have fish, meats, and many other dishes. Perhaps, they are not the best for the gourmet, but they are very good, and prices are reasonable."

"That works for me. I'll be back in a jiffy."

"I do not know this word 'gee-fee.'"

"It means fast."

After Buster had gone, Marie turned the screens back on and she and Quint resumed studying the images that flicked past. After his return with the food, Buster resumed watching his assigned monitor. The three of them ate and shared the bottle of wine, never taking their focus from the rolling screens. An hour later found them still focused on the monitors.

Quint was almost ready to give up, when Marie whispered as though to herself, "Hmm." Both he and Buster looked at her monitor as she put it on pause. There on the screen was the image of Rene handing a large bundle to two men, one heavy set and older, the younger tall and thin. The bundle was wrapped in a cover of some kind so it was impossible to say what it might be, but judging from the size and the weight, it could well be a body. Quint asked, "Can you zoom in on the image?"

Marie instantly complied. Quint nodded his head as he studied the monitor. "I need a copy of the image to forward to the CIA along with the time frame this section was recorded. Is that possible?"

"Of course, that is simple. Should I also notify the police of this tape?"

"Thank you. It might help their own investigation into Rene Gaston's murder."

By the time they left the Port Authority office, it was after ten o'clock. Both men were past weary as they walked along the quay towards their hotel. As they walked, Quint phoned Gerald.

He immediately rushed into his reason for the early call, "Gerald, we found a camera monitor at the port that has several minutes showing Rene Gaston, the murdered shop owner, handing over a body-sized package to two men. I am forwarding the image to you to see if you can identify the men. Also, it would be helpful to pull up satellite images of the port showing the boat and when it left port."

"That's not a problem. I'll pull satellite imagery of the boat and track it. We can determine where it makes port and who gets off. Keep in touch if you learn anything more there. Until then, I'll do what I can on the satellite angle and get back to you as soon as we know something."

"Thanks, Gerald. With the technology available in the Agency, I hope your guys can find where they are taking her."

"You may be premature about the boat. Don't get your hopes too high. This might not be Lila in that package at all."

"I understand what you are saying, but my gut tells me otherwise."

Quint rang off and the two men walked the remaining distance to the hotel in silence. When they collected their keys from the desk, Buster said, "I think I will follow up with Marie. Chat her up and see if she knows any gossip that would lead us to why Gaston would get involved in a kidnapping."

Quint smiled, "That's not a bad idea. By the way, I noticed the looks you two exchanged when we said goodnight to her. I think there were some sparks flying. Don't let it get in the way of our mission though."

"No way. But there's no reason not to mix a little pleasure with business until we know what to do next."

Chapter 5

Lila stumbled after Smokey. She could not keep the alarm from her voice when she asked, "Where are you taking me?"

Smokey snarled in reply, "We are landing shortly. We are handing you off to someone else. You are not my problem after that, lady."

"Where are we? Who is it you are taking me to?"

He ignored her questions. When they reached the steps to the deck, he ordered, "Climb."

Terrified, Lila shook her head, "No. Not until you tell me where you are taking me."

"Climb up the fucking steps or I'll drag you up. I don't give a damn how you get up there, but you're going up."

"Jackass," Lila murmured under her breath as she climbed. When she reached the top step, Chef gave her his hand and helped her the rest of the way up. She shivered in the early morning air, her silk sundress offering little protection against a stiff wind. Chef noticed, and in a moment handed her a jacket still warm with body heat. She accepted it gratefully.

"Thank you so much." She smiled. The very fact that he gave her his jacket assured her that he, at least, meant her no harm. He took her elbow and guided her to a seat at the side of the cockpit. Close to the cabin wall, the seat offered some shelter from the wind. Hoping that Smokey could not hear, she whispered to Chef, "Can you tell me where you are taking me?"

He whispered in reply, "I am sorry, signora. I cannot do that."

Lila bit her lip and nodded.

In some minutes, she felt the engine slowing down. Wherever they were taking her, she suspected she would soon know. She could hear the murmur of voices off to her right. It sounded like two men, but with the noise of the engine, wind, and waves she could not determine what they were saying. Lila shivered again. This time it was the cold fingers of fear creeping down her spine and not the temperature. She could only hope that whoever these men were, they would not kill her before she could either be rescued or escape. As it was, she wished that she could suddenly become invisible.

There was a soft bump as the boat nudged against a dock. Pulling her to her feet, Smokey picked her up and handed her off to one of the men on the dock. There the man stood her on her feet, keeping a tight hold of her elbow. He snapped, "Don't do anything stupid. I'm not in the mood for it."

Lila was pondering a response, when a sudden shot rang out followed by a thud.

"No, por favore..." Chef's voice was cut off by a second shot. Again, she heard the sound like a body hitting some surface. Lila swallowed the scream that welled up from deep inside. Tears ran unchecked down her face as she sobbed silently. She could not stop trembling and hated that the man holding her arm could feel her shaking. Although Chef and Smokey had brought her to this place, they had not harmed her. She had not particularly liked Smokey, but she hated the thought of him being shot. Chef's death hit even harder as he had been kind to her. He was a young man with hopes. She could only wonder what had led him into a criminal enterprise and said a silent prayer for his soul. She wondered, when they had what they wanted from her, if she would face the same fate.

The man that was gripping her arm, ordered the other man, "Start the engine of that boat and put it in gear. Take it out a couple of hundred feet and pour some gasoline on the deck, not too much, but enough to keep burning. Jump overboard once the fire gets going. When the fire hits the engine, it's going to explode. You need to swim back as fast as you can. You want to be well away from the boat when it goes. I'll take the woman to the car and we will wait for you."

"Shit. Why is it that I'm the one that always gets the dirty work?"

The man laughed at the comment as he dragged Lila to a car parked nearby. The next hour was a nightmare for her. She had no idea the identity of the men who had taken her, but thought she detected a faint Slavic or perhaps Russian accent in the voice of the one who had taken the boat back out. Whoever they were they were seriously evil. She felt her nose running from the tears, but with hands now tied, she had no way to stop it. Leaning to the side she wiped it on her upper arm before leaning back in the seat. In the distance, she could hear the engine of the boat as it went back out to sea. It was not long before a distant boom told her that her two earlier captives were held within the arms of the deep for an eternity. The man said nothing to her as she sat in the car waiting. She could hear him in the distance talking on a phone, but nothing of the conversation was clear enough to register the words. She desperately needed to relieve herself. The adrenalin pumping through her system had her kidneys on overdrive.

Hating the very necessity of it, Lila called to the man, "Please, can you untie me and lead me somewhere private? I desperately need to urinate."

He did not reply, but she could hear his feet crunching on the sand as he approached and opened her door. "Get out."

Lila hurried to oblige his order. When she was out of the car, he undid the bindings at her wrist and led her several paces away. "Do not remove the blindfold. Do your business and be done with it."

"Would you please look the other way?"

"What's the matter? You think I want to see your bare ass?"

"I don't know what you want. All I know is that I want to go back to my husband and forget this ever happened."

"Lady, that's not possible. Get on with it so I can get your hands tied and get you back in the car. My partner will be back any minute, and we have to leave." His voice was cruel when he laughed. "You have no schedule, but we do. Now shut up and pee."

Lila relieved herself and then allowed the man to retie her hands. She could sense that he had watched and enjoyed her humiliation. Before she could stop herself, she blurted, "Why did you have to kill those men? Are you going to kill me, too? If you are, why do you think I would do anything you want?"

He chuckled, "Have you never heard dead men don't talk? Neither do dead women. You will do what the boss wants, bitch, or you will regret it and beg to die."

"If that's the case, just kill me now."

"And miss out on payday? I don't think so."

"You are an American. I can tell by your voice. Why would you do this?"

"Money!"

Any further conversation was ended as the other man

reached shore and walked towards them. She heard him open the trunk of the car and then close it. At least she was not going to have to ride in there, she thought. Several minutes later, the man got in behind the wheel and said to the man that had held her by the arm. "Let's get this done and over with."

Shoving her into the car, he said, "That's fine with me."

Again, Lila could not stop a shiver of fear. They had just casually murdered her earlier captors. What did they have in store for her? For the next hour the three of them rode in a silence broken only by the sound of the engine, the purr of the wheels on pavement, and a breeze from the sea. She could tell by the curves in the road that moved her body from side to side and from the popping in her ears that they were in mountainous terrain. Her knowledge of geography from school days was no help without an origination reference point. She could only judge that they had traveled some 15 or so hours by boat from the port in Cassis to where she was transferred to these two men who were far more brutal than the last two. For the moment, she dared say not say anything. It seemed important to her to wait and hope they would talk and give her a clue for what was in store for her. Good or bad, there was nothing more she could do at this point to help herself. She would have liked to ask that the bindings that hurt her wrists be removed. She would like to ask for the blindfold to be taken off. She suspected neither would happen no matter how she begged. So, she sat mute. Closing her eyes, she tried deep breaths to force herself to relax. In time, the shaking that transmitted her fear to her captor stopped.

At some point she must have dozed. The car came to a stop, waking her from sleep. The man behind the wheel said that he was going to get three coffees and something to eat as they still had a long drive ahead to reach their destination. The man that sat beside her in the back seat told him to go ahead. She waited until the driver returned with the coffee and food. Both thirsty and hungry, she accepted it with gratitude. Lila bit into the crunchy almond croissant. It had been hours since she had eaten, and the food was welcome. She greedily drank down the rich cappuccino. Both men had eaten before she finished, and the man beside her had gone inside to use the facilities.

Lila asked the driver, "I'm sorry. No one asked me, but I really need to use the restroom. Please, allow me to go."

"No can do. If I take that blindfold off, we'll have to kill you. Lady, you are smart enough to know I can't let you march in there with your hands tied and wearing a blindfold. After we reach a spot I can pull over, you can get out and go in the bushes. That's the best I can offer."

Frustrated, Lila sat back in the seat. Her chance for escaping before reaching whatever destination they had in mind, had just vanished. The second man came back to the car and this time climbed in front with the driver. At least that was some relief to her. She had hated having him sit close beside her. At times she had felt his thigh brush her leg making her cringe. It was bad enough to be kidnapped, but rape would make it even worse. Sometime later, Lila felt the car slowing as the driver pulled off the road.

The driver commented, "She said she needs to pee. I'm going to untie her hands and walk her behind those bushes. Once she's finished, how about you take the last leg of the trip. I'm tired."

Lila bit her lip when the other man responded, "I'll take her."

"Naw, it's all right. I'll take her while you get in the driver's seat."

Lila breathed a sigh of relief when the driver opened the door and helped her to stand by the car. "I'm going to untie your hands, but that blindfold stays on."

Taking her arm, he led her several yards from the car and told her he would turn his back while she relieved herself. Lila hastened to do as ordered. Deciding he was the nicer of the two and hoping to play on his better nature, she asked. "These bindings hurt my hands. Could you please leave them off? It's not as though I can go anywhere with two of you watching me. For that matter, I don't even know where we are."

"Just finish your business. I'll see about your hands, but you'd better not pull anything funny. My partner would just as soon kill you as not."

Lila shivered from the cold as she adjusted her clothes. Crossing her fingers, she said, "I'm finished. I understand and I won't try anything."

He guided her as they walked back to the car. Opening the door, he ordered her to get in. Lila was relieved that the driver had not noticed that her hands were still untied. Turning the heater on, the driver commented that it was getting colder as they climbed. That confirmed her earlier suspicion that they were in the mountains. The two men talked little as they continued to their destination.

On feeling the warmth of the car and lulled by the noise of the tires as they bore her onward, Lila dozed off. When the gentle whirr of the tires on pavement was replaced by the harsher sound of cobbles or rocks beneath the car, Lila stirred and sat up from her slumped position. Surely, they must be nearing the destination. She became aware of the car slowing and coming to a halt, the engine still running. The driver lowered his window and spoke to someone outside. The car shifted back into gear and moved forward. She could hear the slow creak of a gate of some kind opening to allow admittance. They had arrived. The thought of what awaited her filled her with terror. Whatever it was, they expected her to do something for them. If she failed, she suspected they would kill her. And if she succeeded at what they wanted, would they allow her to live? She took a deep breath to prepare herself as the car rolled to a stop. This was it.

She heard the two front doors of the car open as her captors exited. The rear door opened, and she was ordered out. Grasped roughly by the elbow, she was pulled from the car. Lila stumbled out. Before she could fall, the driver hoisted her upright and took her by the elbow. She walked over what felt like cobbles beneath her feet. There was a piercing wind blowing. She could hear it rustling nearby trees and howling around the eaves of a dwelling. With no choice but to face what awaited her, she walked stoically forward.

A man greeted the three of them. His voice was deep, brusque with a cultured overtone. He wasted no time, saying, "Good. You men may collect your pay. You know the routine. After that get lost for a few weeks. I'll let you know if I need you again."

"Sure, boss." It was the driver that replied.

Lila stood still awaiting what would happen next. The man spoke to her, softening his voice, "Miss Carson, thank you for joining me here."

"I'm married. The name is Lila Carson Cord," Lila snapped.

"My apologies...Mrs. Cord. I so look forward to working with you."

Lila gaped at his words. It was bizarre for him to act as

though she was some long-awaited guest. Not sure what to say, she said nothing.

"Ah, well. Not very talkative, are you? Allow me to take your arm and lead you into my little mountain home. I trust you will be comfortable here."

Lila felt her mouth twitch and could not stop the words that tumbled out, "Lovely, now, if you would be so kind as to show me to my accommodations and permit me to call my husband, I would be most grateful."

The man's laugh was deep and genuine, "I do like a spirited woman. The first I can do; however, you will not be calling your husband."

Chapter 6

"Quint," Gerald said, "Our satellite is on it. We have film footage of someone loading a package onto a boat in the harbor of Cassis. We tracked the boat to a small harbor near Spezia on the North Coast of Italy. There they took a woman and put her into a car. Zoomed in on, it appears to be Lila. The two men that took her from Cassis were shot and the boat taken out to sea and exploded. We now have a satellite tracking the car north. It appears they are heading toward Switzerland, but we cannot be sure at this point. As soon as we have something more, I will get back to you."

"Thank you, Gerald. It is such a relief to know she is all right so far. I think Buster and I are going to begin traveling towards northern Italy, so we are close by if you get a destination."

"That's fine. There's little more that you can do in Cassis. The local police are on the case of the murdered shop owner, and my agents there are tracking the purveyance of the motor yacht that the men used to take Lila from there to Italy. As soon as they find the owner, I'll let you know. I suspect it will not be helpful as it may well belong to some bogus corporation. At any rate, we hope to know more soon."

"I'll keep you posted as to our whereabouts."

Gerald laughed, "No need, we know where you are and when you move, we will have a view of that, too."

"Geez. I should have known. There's no privacy in this world anymore."

"Come on, it's not that bad. You guys are ours, so it is only natural for us to keep track and look out for you," Gerald replied.

"Is there a chance you can upload that live satellite feed to my phone?"

"That shouldn't be a problem. I'll have a technician get on that for you."

Quint ended the call and turned to Buster. "Let's pack and check out. We're about to take a little road trip."

"So, I gathered from your conversation with Gerald. I'll be ready in ten. You?"

"It will take me a little longer. I've got to pack both my things and Lila's. Why don't you check us out while I'm packing; and I'll meet you in the lobby. The front desk has my credit card, and Gerald was going to call to handle your charges. You will probably just need to pick up the paperwork for Agency records."

"Sure, no problem. I'll see you downstairs in a few."

It took Quint only minutes to pack his items into his large bag. When he began to pack Lila's things, he had to stop and take a calming breath. It hurt to handle the things she had bought so lovingly for her honeymoon, never imagining that it would end with her abduction. It scared him that she might not live to use any of her beautiful trousseau again. When he had carefully packed her belongs, he snapped the case shut, locked it, and called for a bellman to come for the bags. Not only did he have the two large bags, but her carry-on, his carry on, and Lila's ever-present computer case. Quint did a final check around the room after the bellman collected his bags. It was a beautiful place to spend a honeymoon; he was just sorry that it ended the way it did.

Within minutes, Buster and Quint were on A57 speeding towards the A8 that would take them past Cannes, Nice and

Monte Carlo on the Haute Corniche. Quint was sorry that Lila was not with him to enjoy the spectacular view of the Mediterranean's rugged coast where mountains sprinkled with small villages drop down into the dazzling blue of the sea. As it was, a delighted Buster enthused over the scenery that flew by the window at a dizzying pace. Quint was so focused on getting closer to Lila that he had time to do nothing but concentrate on his driving. He was barely aware of either the view or Buster's comments. They stopped at a service area near Genoa, used the restroom, bought gas, and grabbed a bite to eat. Quint opened Lila's laptop, tethered it to his phone, and found the live satellite feed Gerald had promised. It did not take him long to spot the car as it moved past Milan still traveling north. Once they were back on the road, they turned north just past Genoa onto the E25 heading toward Milan. With Buster monitoring the satellite feed, they should have no trouble following the car that carried Lila.

Just north of Milan, Buster cried, "Bingo! The car just stopped. It looks like a gated estate to the north of Lugano. I can see them taking Lila into what appears to be one damned big house. According to the map, it is just outside of Gandria, and right on the lake. It looks like there's a boat dock with a power boat tied to it. I suspect this place is no more than a twenty-minute drive from Lugano."

"Stay on it. I'm going to phone Gerald for back up."

"Good idea."

Quint phoned Gerald to ask for two sniper rifles, two sets of night vision goggles, and two tasers. He also wanted to know anything they could learn about the estate and its owner. Gerald informed him his agents were already working on that and that he had arranged for an operative to meet them at the Grand Hotel

Splendide Royal on the lake front in Lugano. All three men would have a reservation at the hotel awaiting their arrival. After the call ended, Quint racked his brain for what he knew about Lugano. Other than being a beautiful and touristic city, the only thing that might have any bearing on this particular locale for whatever they planned for Lila was either the banks of Lugano or the proximity to Campione D'Italia. Lugano served as a tax haven for European citizens, and Campione D'Italia as a gambling mecca for Italians who could not legally gamble in Italy. The reason for this site would have to await more information from Gerald.

Quint had been to the Grand Hotel Splendide years before on a vacation with his parents. It was not difficult for him to find it on the main drive around the lake that curved from Campione D'Italia on the right side of the lake to the town of Lugano on the left. Done in the style of bygone grandeur, the elegant hotel reception area was large and ornate. Quint and Buster found their adjoining rooms with a sitting room between already booked. Located on the front of the hotel with views of the lake visible from their rooms, both men gravitated to their window and took a moment to enjoy the sparkling water. Across the road from the hotel, a park with benches and an ambling walkway led to the downtown area on the right of the hotel, no more than ten minutes away.

After they had unpacked the bare necessities, Quint met Buster in the sitting room where they immediately hooked up their laptops and logged on to the satellite feed. They could detect no movement of the car during the time they had been checking in. Although there was some interference with their view of the estate due to trees and shrubbery, it appeared that the entire grounds were surrounded by a wall. As they watched, a man leading...what they took to be dogs, left the main house and started to walk around the perimeter of the estate.

"Well, that answers one question. It's guarded. The man with the dogs is probably armed as well. Let's keep watching to see if he is the only one on guard duty." Quint leaned towards the laptop screen as he talked, studying it for any detail that might prove useful. As he watched, he toyed with an idea that would let Lila know he was nearby.

Quint picked up the phone, ignoring the late hour in Washington.

Gerald had obviously been sleeping when he answered. Clearing his throat, he asked, "Yeah, Quint. What do you need that can't wait for morning?"

"Look, I'm sorry, but until Lila is safe, I damned well can't sleep. I just thought of something. I want to let her know that I'm nearby, and I need to know which room of that house she is being held in. Could you have our guys develop a short commercial featuring Lugano as a honeymoon destination and saying something about the lights are always on there. If we could get internet users in Ticino province to get the message when they log on, it would accomplish both goals: Lila would know I am here, and she could leave the light on at night in her room so I will know in which room of the house they are holding her."

"Damn. You know Quint, I think that might work. It's 5:00 AM here. I will be in the office in three hours and get our agents to contact the internet provider for the province of Ticino to allow the commercial to pop up the minute anyone logs on. I have some guys on staff that can put together what you need in minutes. We can assure the Ticino area that it is only a short-term interruption of their normal system. The minute Lila is forced to log on, she should see and understand the message. If it doesn't work, we will see what else we can figure out from here." Gerald paused, "Did our asset there contact you?"

"No. We've heard nothing from anyone."

"I'll get on that in the morning. He should already have been in contact with you."

"Okay. Keep me posted." Quint rang off and looked at Buster. "There's not much we can do until Gerald gets that commercial posted and the local agent shows up. What say we get something to eat? If I remember correctly, the hotel restaurant makes a great spaghetti carbonara."

"That works for me."

"Salad and a bottle of wine to go with it?"

"Sure. I'll phone room service with our order."

"Thanks, Buster." Quint leaned back in the Empire style chair and studied the ceiling. If he could determine in which room they were holding Lila, he should be able to figure out a way to free her. He returned his attention to the laptop where the grounds of the villa were on live feed. With nothing else to do while they awaited the delivery of food, Quint pulled out a notepad and readied his pen. Any small detail could prove vital. He had never been more grateful for modern technology than he was at that moment. Somewhere in that villa was his wife, the woman he loved and finally had the courage to claim. He could not help wondering if his love for her and pride in her ability were not the very reason that she was now in captivity at the hands of some unknown person or persons. What was it they wanted from her, and if they got it, would they allow her to live? Quint broke out in a cold sweat just thinking about it. Somehow, he had to free her before they could activate their plans.

Buster and Quint enjoyed their meal. However, sitting with the computer open on the table where both could see, they were distracted by the images on the laptop. With the meal finished and the cart rolled into the hall for pick up, they returned to the computer.

"Buster let's start timing the circuit this guy with the dogs makes. At some point, he is going to be relieved if they keep up an all-night surveillance of the grounds. I feel certain they must, but we need to know when that happens. I would love to know how many other guards are on the property and where they are stationed. Let's see if we can zoom in and detect security cameras. It makes sense they would have them. If they are there, we need to see if Gerald's people can deactivate them, or if there is some way we can get a message to Lila to do it. We stand a better chance of snatching her if we know we aren't on a monitor from the minute we enter the grounds."

"Yeah. You are right. Hey, look…there by the rear of the property. It looks like there's another guy patrolling. I didn't see him before, so I don't know if he's been there all along or just coming on duty."

"Where?"

"There by that tree." Buster pointed at the guard who was also leading a dog on a chain.

Quint nodded. "You're right. He could have been hidden by the trees and been there all along, and we just missed him. Let's see if there is a pattern to his patrol and how long each circuit takes."

"Okay. You watch and time the one in front and I'll do the same for the one in the rear of the estate."

Both men scribbled notes as they tried to discern both pattern and timing for the two guards. An hour into their focus on the guards, they were interrupted by the phone on the sofa table. Quint went to answer the phone as Buster continued making notes for the guy he was watching and trying to keep a cursory monitoring of the guard in front. He was so intent, he noticed nothing of the phone conversation. After several minutes, Quint walked back to the laptop and sat down.

"That was the local CIA legate. He had to drive up from Milan, so he is just getting here and checking in now. He will be up as soon as he's settled.

Twenty minutes later, both men looked up at the knock on the door. Buster stood, "I'll get it. Must be the guy from Milan."

Buster opened the door to a pint-sized little man with owl like glasses perched on the end of a pinch nose. Sparkling blue eyes, round rosy cheeks, and sparse hair sticking up in all directions completed the image of a merry little elf. A briefcase, half as big as he, hung from one shoulder which dropped lower by the second as he stood there. Buster forced himself not to gape and waited for the man to introduce himself.

He wasted no time, "Get your chin up off the floor, man. I may not look too tough, but I know how to take care of myself. Name's Freddy, Frederick Dickens to be exact."

"Pleased to meet you, Fred. I'm Buster Walton." The two shook hands before Buster added, "And who did you say you work for?"

"I didn't. But I think Director Williams told you to expect me."

"That's right, he did. Come on in. The guy over there glued to the computer is Quint Cord. His wife is the woman that was abducted."

"Terrible, that." Freddy walked over to Quint and stuck out

his hand. "I'm Freddy. Nobody calls me Fred. I don't like it."

Buster and Quint each caught the other's eye, and both stifled the impulse to grin. "I'm pleased to meet you, Freddy. So, tell me what the Director told you and how you plan to help us."

An hour later Freddy was still talking…even while all three men stared at the computer screen, with Quint and Buster taking notes on the activity of the guards. Finally, Freddy exhausted the flow of words and he too silently studied the screen. After thirty minutes, Freddy opened his briefcase and pulled out his own laptop. He hurriedly got it plugged in and up and running. Quint and Buster glanced up as his fingers flew across the keyboard at a staccato pace. Both men shrugged their shoulders and returned to the monitor they were studying. Another hour went by, interrupted only by the scratching of Buster and Quint's pens as they made notes and the intermittent noise of Freddy tapping away on his computer keyboard. Suddenly, the little legate looked up and announced. "I may have something."

Instantly alert, Quint turned to him, "What have you got?"

"This property you are monitoring belongs to Lyon Alexander Owens, an international playboy who made his money years ago in currency trading. Since then he has invested his capital in various ventures. Most turned out well for him, but one turned into a stinking nightmare and lost him a bundle. Seems he invested in the Casino in Campione D'Italia which has gone belly up. I don't know what he is up to, or why he took your wife, but it may have something to do with that."

"See if you can find out where he banks and what kind of assets remain in the Casino property that he might be able to go after?"

"I'm already on it."

Chapter 7

Although Lila could not see to admire it, she walked into a luxurious Louis XIV style foyer. Gold gilding lit up the woodwork; gold tassels ornamented heavy dark green draperies topped by gilded pelmets. The marble floor, polished to a high sheen, was softened by thick oriental carpets. A curving marble stair, with iron fretwork banisters, led into a landing lit by a huge ormolu window.

"Allow me to show you to your chambers and get settled. I think you will find my staff has provided anything you may need in the way of personal effects. If not, please let me know and I will see what we can do."

"By any chance, did you replace the cell phone your hired thug tossed in the sea?"

"You do have a sense of humor." His words were followed by another deep laugh.

Lila shrugged her shoulders with resignation as he led her up the stairs. He stopped at a door on the far-left end of a long hallway that branched off on both sides of the upper landing. "Once you are inside, you may remove your blindfold and make yourself comfortable. You will be taking your meals here so you will not have the discomfort of eating with a blindfold on. When there is a knock on the door, replace the blindfold securely. If at any time you should see one of us, we will be forced to dispense with your services…and of course, you as well."

"Of course. And, just why should I believe that once I have done whatever it is you expect of me, you are going to let me go?"

"I have a love for all things beautiful. You are a beautiful woman, as well as a talented one. I have no desire to see your demise. I will not hesitate, however, in the interest of my own self-protection to eliminate any threat to me. So, be very careful to follow instructions, and I will let you go unmolested when I am through with you."

"I am supposed to trust you!?"

Again, that deep laugh, "You have no real choice, now do you?"

"As you say." Lila turned on her heel and faced away from the direction of his voice. A moment later she heard the door to the room close and the soft click of a key turning in the keyhole.

Lila slowly counted to sixty before lifting the blindfold and looking around her prison. It was the ultimate of tasteful luxury. Obviously designed for a woman, the room was decorated with gilded Louis XVI chairs and a desk that were placed before double French doors that led onto a balcony. Lila hurried to try the doors, only to find them securely locked. Upholstered in pale cream with rose and lime green stripes, the bed was framed on either side and behind the carved headboard, by a rose-colored drape edged by the same green hue as in the stripes. She plumped the bed with her hand and smiled at the feel of the comfortable sleep it promised. Still exploring the room, she walked over to an armoire beside a door leading into a pink marble bathroom. Lila opened the armoire and gasped as she looked through dresses, blouses, skirts, gowns, and robes...all in her size. On one side of the huge armoire, another door opened to reveal drawers holding shoes and undergarments...again in her size. She thoughtfully closed the door and walked into the marble floored bath. Mirrored walls reflected her image on all sides. Mirrored doors opened to disclose a commode and bidet closet on one side, and a well-stocked linen closet on the other. Opening the cabinets and drawers, she discovered lotions, makeup, toiletries, and other women's essentials. On the pink marble counter, Paris designer perfume bottles sparkled in the light from a crystal chandelier. Someone had foreseen every possible need. The thoroughness of the preparations was eerie. Lila could only surmise that they planned for a prolonged period of capture or she was occupying the room of the owner's mistress. The only positive seemed to be that they must not be planning to murder her immediately. She could only hope the interim would give her time to either escape or be rescued.

Lila returned to the armoire, pulled out a silk and lace confection of a bathrobe and returned to the bathroom. At any other time, she would have paused to admire the lavish garment, but at the moment a hot shower sounded heavenly. She turned on the taps and soon had a stream of hot water spraying from the large showerhead. Shedding the clothes that she had worn since her abduction, she dropped them to the floor and stepped in. When she emerged with hair dripping and skin pink from the heat, she felt as though she was ready to face whatever came next. After toweling, she wrapped herself in the robe and combed her hair. In one of the drawers she found a curling iron and a dryer.

Thirty minutes later she walked into the bedroom and seated herself in the delicate chair by the window. She was hungry and thirsty. Now, she could only wait, and hope that they would bring her something soon. With the shadows lengthening on the lawn, it would shortly be night fall. As Lila stared out the window, she could spot guards circling the property with dogs. Dogs…she shuddered. They could tear her apart even if she managed to escape her luxurious prison and the guards didn't shoot her. She pulled the drape, shutting out the menacing sight. She had just returned to her chair when a phone that she had not noticed before rang. Walking to the bedside, she picked it up and waited.

"Mrs. Cord, please go into the bathroom and close the door. I will be there in five minutes with your dinner. I will also bring a menu of tomorrow's meals. If there is anything you do not care for, please make note on the menu. After your dinner is delivered, you will have one hour to finish your meal. I will come for the tray after you are once again in the closed bathroom. Do you understand?"

"Yes, thank you." The woman's voice sounded soft and polite. Perhaps there was some way that Lila could persuade her to help.

In exactly five minutes, the knock alerting Lila that her meal had arrived sounded. Lila hurried into the bathroom and closed the door. Leaning against the door with her ear tight against it, she waited for the sound of the outer door closing as the woman left. When she heard the door close, Lila emerged from the bathroom to find an ornate silver tray on the table by the window. On it were two bottles of water, a half bottle of wine, a green salad, roasted chicken and vegetables. She salivated at the smell of the beautifully arranged food. Lila wasted no time pouring the water and wine into the glasses and digging into her meal. It was as good as the aroma promised.

When she was finished eating, she sipped the rest of the wine. Placing the water bottles by the bed, she returned to the tray and picked up the menu. Everything on it sounded like cuisine catered by the best of four-star restaurants. Lila chuckled; at least she was in the most luxurious prison anyone had ever devised. Using the pen that lay beside the menu, she quickly jotted down her approval just as the phone rang reminding her to go to the bathroom.

After the tray had been collected, Lila returned to the armoire to look for nightclothes. She pulled out the lacy, silky and transparent night things more appropriate for a bordello than her current situation. At last in despair, she found two of the least revealing nightgowns and pulled them both on. That done, she climbed into bed too exhausted to wonder if such revealing nightwear had been chosen for her. It was not long before she was deep in sleep.

She could not have said how long she had slept or what had awakened her to a room lit only by feeble moonlight. She only knew she was not alone. She kept her eyes closed, barely daring to breathe as she waited. The minutes seemed like hours before she heard the soft click of the door closing followed by the sound of the key turning in the lock. Troubled by the nocturnal visit and the possible motivation behind the racy gowns in the armoire that she was now perforce wearing, Lila spent the rest of the night in restless twilight slumber too afraid to fall into deep sleep. She wondered if they were monitoring her by a hidden camera, where it might be hidden, and whether she had any privacy from prying eyes. She could only wonder at the meaning of it all and what her abductor intended. Whatever they were up to, she would find the camera or cameras and disable them. She would rather deal with their anger than feel eyes on her every moment.

She was up and dressed when the telephone rang announcing the arrival of her breakfast. Grabbing the blindfold, she put it on and stood waiting. When the woman had left, Lila removed the blindfold and picked at the breakfast. It looked delicious, but she had no appetite. As she sat, she allowed her eyes to study the room looking for anything that might hide a surveillance camera. Frustrated that nothing stood out, she pushed her breakfast away and walked to the window. When the woman returned for the tray, Lila kept her back to her.

"You have eaten no breakfast. Are you unwell?"

Lila did not turn around and did not answer.

"You should eat. I will return in a couple of hours and bring you a snack. Perhaps, you will be hungry by then."

Again, Lila refused to turn or answer. After a moment of silence, she heard the door close and the key turning in the lock. Ripping off the blindfold she began a slow circuit of the room. First, she checked the furniture, but finding nothing, she turned to the wall. The patterned wallpaper was distracting. Starting at the right side of the door, she began sliding her hand over the wall to try and detect any irregularity. After a moment she stopped. She could not reach as high as she wished. She debated getting a chair. Deciding it was wiser to continue searching as high as she could reach and then down to waist height would be wiser. Surely any camera would need to be at some height in order to cover the room. When she had completed the lower circuit, she hauled a chair to the door and began again searching the wall for any clue that something might be hidden. She had almost reached the far corner when the phone rang. Abandoning the search, she hastened to answer it.

"Mrs. Cord, you are a clever woman. However, I would suggest you stop looking for whatever it is you're seeking."

"You know damned well what I'm looking for, you perverted bastard. Do you think I enjoy being spied on by you? It's bad enough that I've been kidnapped; must you deprive me of any privacy as well?"

His voice was unperturbed when he answered, "You are in a bit of a mood this morning. I had hoped the luxury of your accommodations and all of the provided amenities would have provided you with some assurance of my hospitality."

"I would sleep in a pig sty to be out of here."

His only response was a deep laugh before he hung up.

Lila cursed to herself as she climbed back onto the chair and resumed searching. She had only reached the first corner when her search was interrupted by the ringing of the phone. For one small moment she considered not answering. Sighing in resignation, she climbed down from the chair and picked up the receiver.

Again, there was a deep chuckle. "Mrs. Cord, you do tend to complicate things. Please put on your blindfold." He hung up without waiting for an answer.

Lila snatched the blindfold from the table where she had tossed it, put it on, and stood by the window as previously…her back to the room. The turning of the key was followed by the door opening and several pairs of footsteps entering the room. She was frightened at what they might do to punish her, but stoically stood her ground and waited. Behind her she could hear what sounded like things being lifted and moved. The urge to peek was almost overwhelming, but she dared not. In a matter of minutes, she heard their feet retreating, followed by the door closing and the key turning to lock her in once more. Removing the blindfold, she said, "Is anyone still here?"

When she got no answer, she turned to see what they had done. Not only had they taken all the chairs, but also a tall wastebasket. The desk where she ate her meals remained, but the sheer size and weight of it assured her she would not be pushing it around to climb on. Discouraged, she sat on the side of the bed. Her stomach growled to remind her she had refused breakfast. Perhaps, if she went on a hunger-strike they would let her go. She shook her head at the idea. If they were as determined as it appeared, they would only force feed her. Lila had no choice except to wait to see what happened next.

She did not wait long. The shrill ringing of the phone interrupted her troubled thoughts. Picking it up, she said, "Yes?"

"Mrs. Cord put on your blindfold. Someone will be coming for you shortly." The woman hung up without waiting for a response.

Lila's hands shook as she tied on the blindfold. For once, she was grateful for it. Surely if they planned to kill her when they came, they would not care if she could see them or not. But where were they taking her? Even with cameras, the elegant room seemed safer than whatever awaited beyond the door.

Chapter 8

Sitting on the waterfront in the town of Lugano, Quint, Buster, and Freddy enjoyed the last of the two bottles of red wine they had downed with dinner. All three were well sated, and for Quint, it was the first time all day that he felt relaxed. It was a beautiful evening with a full moon hanging overhead and reflected in the tranquil surface of the lake. Freddy took a gulp of his wine, pushed back from the table, crossed his legs, and gave his dinner companions a hard look.

Quint and Buster glanced at one another while they waited to hear what he had to say.

Freddy began, "How much do you know about banking here in Switzerland?"

Buster shrugged and turned to Quint who replied, "Not much. I never had any real reason to know anything about it. Government contracts don't pay that kind of money and most of what I inherited from my parents is in trusts and investment accounts that pay me monthly dividends."

"I see. Well, if Lyon keeps his money in a Swiss bank which would make sense since he has a house here, then we have a slim chance of finding it."

Buster interrupted, "Why do you say slim?"

"The accounts are recognized by numbers known only to the bank and the account holders. The funds are not held under names; furthermore, some have the additional security of a passcode."

"Crap!" Quint took a sip of his wine before asking, "So, if that is the case, how do we find out anything on his bank accounts? Wouldn't it be better if we checked out the casino's assets first to see if there is anything in their accounts he can drain? I think that should be easier."

"I agree. That's public record. I can pull that up when we get back to the hotel. Once that's done, I'm hitting the sack. I've had a long day."

"Trust me, we have, too," Quint responded. "A couple of long days without much sleep for that matter…"

The men paid their tab and walked back to the hotel too tired to enjoy the view of the moon sparkling on the lake. None of them wasted any time getting to bed. While Buster and Freddy were soon sleeping soundly, Quint spent another restless night worrying about Lila. It was a relief to leave his bed at dawn, put on his jogging shoes, and leave the hotel. The run along the shores of the lake allowed him the needed release of days of frustration and helplessness. After thirty minutes, he returned to the hotel, showered, and ordered room service breakfast. He was munching on a flakey croissant and waiting for his computer to fire up when the ad that Gerald had arranged came on the television screen. He nodded his head with approval, took a sip of coffee, and with his eyes squinted, focused on the task at hand. So far as he knew, Freddy's tracking of Lyon Owens' computer did not indicate that as yet Lila had been utilized to hack into something. The longer that remained so, the more uneasy he became. Surely, that was the only reason she had been snatched. If not, he was at a loss to come up with another reason. The more he thought about it, the more troubled he was as to a method for extracting her from the villa where she was being held. After several minutes of deep thought, he checked his watch. It was too early to call Gerald.

A knock on his door interrupted his contemplations. He walked over, checked the peephole, and opened it to allow entry to both Buster and Freddy. After several minutes of inconsequential chatter, Quint turned to Freddy, "Gerald has that ad running, but that is not enough. Do you have access to a heat sensitive radar drone? Even if Lila keeps her light on tonight to indicate which room she is in, I noticed some of those windows are barred. It stands to reason that she would be in one of those rooms. Getting her out through a window would be impossible in any case. We will have to go in another way. That makes it imperative we know exactly where everyone…not just Lila…is in that villa."

"I'll call my office and see if they can get a drone up here." Freddy motioned towards the computer that Quint had opened on his desk. "You got anything yet?"

Quint shook his head.

Seeing how downcast his friend was, Buster said, "It doesn't make a damn bit of difference to me whether Lila gets on that computer or not, we are going to get her out of there. You hang in there, buddy. With us on the case, it's just a matter of time." Buster projected confidence for all he was worth, but inside he just wasn't sure. With no ransom note, it had to be something to do with her special expertise. The fact that several men had died in the process of her abduction to protect the identity of whomever had taken her, made him even more uncomfortable.

"Right. So, what can we do in the meantime?" Quint shrugged his shoulders as he asked, hoping his despair wasn't too obvious.

"I was up for a while last night," Freddy responded. "So far there has been no unauthorized attempt to access the casino accounts that I can tell. I think I found a lead on Lyon's Swiss accounts, as well. If either the casino accounts or Lyon's are accessed, I should know if it is legitimate based on the software used to signature-cloak. Then I'll try to track the IP address of the hacker. We will have to hope that Lila will leave clues. In the meantime, here is a list of the 200 investors in the casino. Some lost money; others appear to have bailed before it collapsed."

"Any assets left?" Quint asked.

"They went belly up with a debt of over one hundred and thirty million Euros. The only asset is the casino, gaming equipment, and furnishings. Used furnishings and equipment bring pennies on the dollar. As for that ugly monstrosity of a casino, there is some dickering going on as to what to do with it. With the loss of jobs and revenue for local businesses, you've got folks screaming all over the canton of Ticino. With over 500 or so unemployed workers and townspeople whose businesses depended on the casino, there is one hell of a lot of bitching going on to get it reopened. It's affected tourism here in Lugano, too. Then you've got Campione itself which has been one hundred percent dependent on the casino for funding. The casino's in the hands of the court in Como with three judges appointed to determine what to do. Politics also come into play. Switzerland has been trying for years to annex Campione, but so far, Italy is unwilling to play ball. At some point, the pressure might be enough for them to cave and turn it over to Switzerland. That is probably the best scenario for the reopening of the casino. In the meantime, there is a 55,000 square meter building over there gathering dust while Campione dries up."

Quint sat in thought for a moment before responding, "It

looks like that dog won't hunt. There must be some other angle we are missing to justify Lila being kidnapped. Until she goes on-line, and we can track her, we are just playing a guessing game."

Buster piped up, "Tell you what, I'm not that savvy with the computer stuff. I'll monitor the guards and see if there is any change in routine or coming and going from the compound."

Freddy added, "As for me, I suspect I'm the computer guru here…even though I may not be in the same league as your wife, Quint. So, I'll monitor Lyon's computer."

Quint stared out the window for long moments before heaving a sigh. "You guys have about covered things here. I guess I'll poke around town and see if I can learn anything about Lyon that might give us a lead. Before I head out, I'm going to call Gerald."

When the phone rang, Gerald's answering machine came on. Quint left him a message to call, told the guys he would see them later and went out into another beautiful day on the lake. It really was a stunningly picturesque area with various attractions worth visiting, including the nearby lakes of Locarno and Bellagio with charming towns clinging to their shorelines and rugged mountains. Charter boats for exploring the Lake of Lugano rode the gentle waves along the shore-walk to downtown. Quint wondered if Lila would ever want to return here as a tourist after the ordeal she was enduring. For that matter, would he?

His cell phone rang, pulling him back to the present. He walked over to an unoccupied bench and sat facing the water as he answered. "Gerald, it looks like we are on the wrong path with the casino angle. I wondered if you would do a search on this Lyon guy and see if you can dig up something that we are missing here. Also, if all else fails and we need to do a black-op extraction, do you have a team nearby that we can put on alert?"

"I'll get my guys started on the digging right away. If there is anything out there, we'll find it. As for the extraction team, I can have what you need in Lugano in a matter of a couple of hours. I'll give our assets a heads-up on that. By the way, I guess you saw the ad?"

"Yes, it was on this morning. If Lila sees it and figures out the message, hopefully she will signal with her light so we will know which room she's in. I also asked Freddy to arrange for a surveillance drone to be sent up from Milan."

"I know, I approved it already. We also have a satellite equipped with infra-red capability monitoring the villa right now. As soon as I get a count on the occupants and their locations in the villa, I'll let you know."

"I thought I would check around Lugano to see if I can learn anything here from the locals. Maybe a former maid or guard that would be willing to talk..."

"Sounds like a plan. Stay in touch and try not to go nuts with worry."

"Yeah, as if."

An hour wandering around Lugano and asking questions yielded nothing useful. Rather than returning to the hotel, Quint hailed a taxi and instructed the driver to take him to the village of Gandria. Quint sorted through what little he knew of the village from his on-line search. Having become a part of Lugano in 2004, the village no longer maintained a separate governance. Apparently, the closest thing to a city center was either a church, Chiesa di San Vigilio, or a small waterfront at the base of the village with a taverna or two. The Lyon villa lay on the right side of the road not too distant from the tunnel that lead to the approach to Gandria. Quint chatted with the driver, Guiseppe Magnani, who spoke fairly good English, and with the closing of the casino, was delighted to give Quint a tour of the area. When they passed the huge wrought iron gates to the villa, Quint pointed to it and casually remarked, "Whoever that is must have a pot of money. Those are some impressive gates!"

"You should see house. It is palace fit for king."

"Have you been in it?" Quint struggled to keep the excitement from his voice.

"Hah, taxi drivers do not get invitation from Signor Owens. No, I took fare from the Royal Excelsior in Lugano…big party. Rolls, Mercedes, Ferraris, you name it. The parking area it full of expensive cars. Guards, too."

"I guess for a big party with all those wealthy guests, guards were a good thing to have."

"Ah, but guards there always. I hear someone try several times to kill owner."

"Any idea why?"

"My sister tell me she think it because of business deal that go bad, but that all she know. She work there as maid, but owner not one to talk much with servants. Pay good, but guards and dogs make her scared all time, especially after she nearly bit by dog."

"I'm a writer. I'm here doing research on the area for a novel. The estate sounds like one I could use in my book. I wonder, would your sister be willing to describe something about it to me? Of course, I would give it a different name. By the way, what is it called?"

"Name is Casa del Lago D'Azurro…that mean in Italian

"house of blue water lake. Lago di Lugano is very blue, as you see. The glacier make lake long time ago. The water it is very clear and very cold even in summer. But it reflect the blue of sky and always it is beautiful."

"It is that." They drove into the tunnel leading to Gandria plunging the car into momentary darkness. Quint noted that Guiseppe had not answered his question about talking to his sister. When they emerged into the light, Quint glanced at his watch. "I see it's time for lunch. Is there a good restaurant in Gandria?"

"Very good. It is near church and the view of lake is wonderful. The food...ah! You love it!" Guiseppe kissed his fingers in appreciation.

"Well, then. You must come as my guest, then we will continue seeing a bit of the area. Okay?"

"With pleasure, Signor Cord. Ristorante Locanda Gandriese will not disappoint."

The driver turned into the small fishing village that descended in stages down the mountainside to boats that lined the lake like a bobbing fringe. When they stopped, Quint noted by the sign out front that the rather plain-fronted restaurant also had rooms for rent. Inside it was equally austere with uncovered dark wooden tables and slatted wooden chairs, but the view was breathtaking. Guiseppe greeted the owner and then waved at the sole waiter, "Mario, I bring you writer who come to see the best of Ticino, so I bring him here."

When Mario came over, Quint was introduced before he led them to a table on the balcony. Along the railing bright geraniums provided a vivid contrast to the blue of the lake and the verdant foliage of the surrounding mountains. The air was fresh and tantalizing aromas wafted from the direction of the kitchen. Quint looked over the flowers to the lake and distant hills and wished that Lila were here with him. For a moment deep sadness washed across his face.

Noticing the somber expression, Guiseppe asked, "Signor Cord, how can such beautiful view make you sad?"

"I was thinking of someone I love very much and wishing she was with me to enjoy the beauty of this place."

"Ah…amore. It is so wonderful to have and so tragic to lose. I myself have felt this many time. Like me, in time you will find there are many beautiful women to make happiness together."

"Are you married, Guiseppe?"

"Yes, but she does not like me so much, so she left. It's okay. I go find amore again. And you, this woman, is she wife or what you call girlfriend?"

"She's my wife and we love each other very much, but she cannot be with me at the moment, so I miss her."

"This time she not here, but you come back with her. Si?"

Quint swallowed to clear the lump in his throat before answering, "I hope so."

Quint picked up his menu and studied it to avoid answering any further questions. Taking the hint, Guiseppe did likewise.

"I recommend prosciutto plate for antipasto. Very good. The fish is from lake and is good, too. But here I like lasagna."

"That sounds fine to me." Quint signaled to Mario who hurried over to take their order.

Bread and a carafe of rosé wine were on the table along with the antipasto within minutes of ordering. Quint ate with relish while they waited for the main course of lasagna for Guiseppe and a seafood risotto for him. With the main dishes he had ordered an arugula salad with shave parmesan. The meal proved to be as delicious as promised, and despite being full, neither man could resist the tiramisu when Mario placed it before them as a compliment of the house.

During the meal, Quint had kept the conversation lowkey to avoid topics he did not wish to delve into while dining. After the tiramisu, both men sipped a limoncello and stared at the lake in silent appreciation, neither anxious to end the peaceful and contented moment. Mario walked over to them when the other customers had all left. Pulling up a chair, he joined them with his own glass of limoncello.

Mario, smiled at Quint, "I hope the food was as good as Guiseppe promised?"

"I can honestly say it is one of the finest meals I have ever had in Switzerland. The view is pretty sensational, too."

"Si, Mario." Guiseppe added, "Now Mr. Cord knows I do not lie about this place even though you and Davide are my friends. I forget to tell him that Gandria is voted one of ten most beautiful villages of Switzerland."

"I can see why. Although I was here on vacation with my parents years ago, we never came to Gandria, only Lugano and Locarno."

"So, Guiseppe," Mario asked, "Is your beautiful sister still working at the Ristorante La Veranda in Lugano? I ask Rosa to dine with me, but she refuses. She is too beautiful to be without a fine man like me in her life. Why do you not put in a good word for me? Tell her I do not chase the women like my friend." Mario winked at Quint as he said it making him smile.

Guiseppe laughed, "I do not do courting for you. Rosa says she wants no man in her life now. My mama is sad we give her no grandbabies. She tell us all days we must marry. What I do? I married, but my wife not give me divorce. She still angry after she see me with Mariella."

"Ah, perhaps your wife wants you back."

"Hah! You see her look knives at me, you know that not true."

Quint leaned back in the chair and smiled to himself. It had not been necessary to do anything more to garner the information he needed about Guiseppe's sister. Mario had done it for him. It was simple good fortune that the Veranda restaurant was in the Splendide Royal. He asked for the check, paid, and was soon in the car while Guiseppe insisted on giving him a tour of the area as promised. Quint would have liked to ask him to take him back to the hotel and skip the tour. He needed to discover what Freddy and Buster had learned and he fully intended to look Rosa up that very afternoon. Deciding there was no point in rushing during the afternoon siesta time, he leaned back in his seat and listened as the driver pointed out the various sites. Perhaps the tour would give him other information he could use.

Chapter 9

The woman holding Lila's elbow stopped. "I am going to open this door. You are to go in. Once you are inside and the door is closed, you may remove your blindfold. Do you understand?"

Lila nodded her head and waited as the woman opened the door and pushed her in. Almost tripping at the sudden shove, she struggled momentarily to regain her balance. The click of the lock in the door at her back reassured her that she could remove the blindfold. Slowly she reached up and untied it. Looking around the room in which she now stood, she could see that it contained the latest in computer equipment, dual screens, and a printer. To the immediate right of the desk where the computer occupied the pride of place was a large mirror. Although she had never seen one, she suspected it was one of those mirrors that allowed an observer to monitor her. On the left was a door. And behind her to the right of the entry was a floor-to-ceiling double doored cabinet. She tossed the wadded-up blindfold onto the desk and waited.

A soft chuckle grated on her nerves. It appeared to come from a speaker over the mirror. She turned towards the mirror as her abductor began to speak.

"Mrs. Cord, while these accommodations are not nearly so luxurious as your previous ones, they will have to do for now. It is time we got down to business. I am sure you are curious as to why you are here and what I need from you. Please, have a seat at the desk. Before I tell you what I need, I would like for you to understand how the necessity for this came to be. Perhaps, then you will not be so harsh in your judgement and so reluctant to help me."

"I suppose you are going to convince me kidnapping and murder are commendable actions?"

Again, the soft chuckle. "Not at all. I am sure we can both agree they are reprehensible. However, if it were your life in danger, would you not take extreme measures to survive?

"Apparently, that is the exact predicament that you have put me in. Either I comply with whatever it is you want, or I die. I find any justification for that a little beyond my comprehension."

"Of course, you do. Now, please make yourself comfortable. You will notice that this office is equipped with the latest technology. If you find you need some software or hardware that is not provided, you have only to tell me. Look around the office. You have seen the mirror and the microphone. I watched you spot them. You must understand this is a necessity. In the room beside yours is my assistant who is proficient in the internet technology. Not with your skills of course, but he's well able to monitor any computer sites you visit or any messages you attempt to send. Do not think for one moment that you can alert someone as to your whereabouts or what we want of you."

Lila cursed under her breath, "Naturally."

The door beside the desk leads into a bathroom. You will find it fully stocked with anything you might require. Should we have omitted something, you need only ask for it."

"Is it also equipped with a camera? If so, I will be damned if I do anything for you."

"Alas, no. However, you cannot blame me for wishing it were. After all, you are a beautiful woman and I enjoy seeing that." He chuckled, "I'm really not as corrupt as you think. Enough of that. On the wall beside the entry door, notice a large cabinet. It contains a Murphy bed."

"I see. This is my new prison. Even with your nasty little cameras, I still prefer the other room better. Besides, I'm like a goldfish in a glass bowl in here."

"I wish that were possible, but what I have in mind for you requires around the clock vigilance."

"I suppose you think I can work all day and all night, day after day? I wouldn't last more than a couple of days; and even then, I would be too sleep deprived to do anything."

"Hence the Murphy bed and the bathroom. I expect you to set up an alert on the computer to tell you when the sites I am interested in are activated and you need to log on."

"And, just why is that?"

"I will explain that as soon as I reveal the reasons for what I need done."

"There is nothing you can say that will justify what you have done."

"Please, don't be so annoying. We do not want me to become angry, I assure you. Be quiet and listen. I will tell a story that may possibly change your opinion of me. It is not my custom to kidnap women. However, when I saw the article in the news, I realized you are perfect for a plan I have been working on."

"There are a lot of people out there with IT skills. Why not just hire one instead of kidnapping me and killing the guys that worked for you in doing it?"

"You are the best according to what I have read. I never deal with less than the best." He paused. His voice was soft but menacing when he continued, "Hear this. You think those guards out there are to keep you from escaping. But, no. They are for my protection. There have been repeated attempts on my life, and I intend to stop it. "

He sucked in a deep breath, "My grandparents, both my grandmother and my grandfather, were Russian aristocrats. When the Tsar was killed, they were forced to flee in the night to escape the revolutionary forces carrying only what they could conceal on their persons. Loyal servants got them to the border of Russia. From there they made their way to Menton, France.

"Perhaps, you know it? It is a lovely little town between Monaco and the Italian border. It was the tradition of my grandparents to summer there in their large villa. Naturally, that was the perfect escape for them. They had some small wealth in the bank in Menton that they kept there for on-going villa expenses and their summer vacation. Plus, they carried with them when they escaped a considerable amount in gold coins, and a fortune in jewels. They were young, in love, and naïve enough to believe that the revolution would fizzle out and they could return to Russia and their former way of life, have their estates restored, and all would be well. It soon became apparent to them that would not happen. They had no job skills: indeed, they had never thought they would need any. So, for a few years, they lived on the money in the bank and the gold coins they had smuggled out. Eventually, they were forced to begin selling my grandmother's jewels.

"My mother, a late in life child, was born during this time. Gradually they were forced to begin letting servants go, but for another year or so managed to hold onto a housemaid, and a nurse for my mother. Then the money ran out. My grandmother was forced to let the servants go and to attempt to run the villa and take care of my mother herself. She had no housekeeping skills, but desperation forced her to learn. My grandfather had begun to sell the jewels to support them, but he realized that like many other Russian aristocrats that had escaped to France, he would have to find work to survive. He knew that the villa, despite being an expense, gave free housing and allowed them to maintain a semblance of their former station in life. It was an elegant building, filled with beautiful antiques. My father decided to turn it into a hotel. They swallowed their pride and opened the villa to the paying public. My mother became both cook and housemaid, my father helped her and managed the business side of things. They were not getting rich, but they were surviving.

"My mother grew up and took over the management of the hotel. They were doing little more than surviving, but as long as they had the villa, they kept their pride, and a sense of their roots. My mother was fluent in French, Russian, Italian, German, and English. That allowed her to mix easily with the guests. Her parents became less and less helpful as they aged, forcing her to hire servants to help with running the hotel. That curtailed the revenue, but still they struggled on. Then the war came. The villa was confiscated by the Nazis, and they were forced to live in the servants' quarters. My grandparents and my mother eventually started to work for the resistance. They were caught, and my mother escaped but my grandparents were tortured and put to death.

"When the war was over, she met an American soldier and married him. With nothing to hold her in France except for the abandoned and damaged villa, they moved to Richmond, Virginia, my father's home. He was handsome and charming, and a total rogue. He gambled any earnings he made, depending on my mother's tutoring of foreign languages to support them. As my mother had been, I was a late in life baby. Neither of my parents were suited for the new role in which they found themselves. The strain became too much, and my father abandoned us when I was sixteen.

"We were poor, but my mother, with her pride in our heritage, kept up the pretense of aristocracy. When my friends came to visit, it soon became a joke as she could not keep from commenting that in Russia, she would be a princess and that she owned a large villa in Menton. My friends laughed behind her back and to my face. I hated the teasing.

"In my senior year, due to my intellectual acumen, I won a scholarship to Harvard. My benefactor was a businessman with a large international corporation. He helped indigent students like me in order to bring them into his business. We were expected to go to work for the company after graduation. We were treated like peons and paid worse. Many left for that reason, but I stuck it out and worked my way up to CFO.

"I was finally making good money and gaining respect in the company, until a Christmas party changed it all. One of the secretaries started flirting with me and asking questions. I was stupid enough to tell her my family history and my mother's maiden name. Soon it was all over the company that I was some kind of Russian royalty. The CEO found out and started to make my life hell. I could not figure out why until one day he let it slip that his family were also Russian. He laughed in my face when he told me that my grandparents held his family like slaves on the family estate where they worked in the fields. He glared at me and cackled that he now owned me."

"Did you quit when he did that?" Lila was enthralled by the story despite herself.

"No. I had a better idea. I had been living frugally because I wanted to restore the estate in Menton. My mother dreamed of living out the last days of her life there. However, after that meeting I changed my immediate goals and became an absolute miser, despite making a substantial six figure income. Slowly I began purchasing stock in the company but never in large enough blocks to alert anyone to what I was doing. I then began courting the Board of Directors and soon had enough support to be voted onto the board. In another year, I owned more stock than the CEO. With the support of the board, I leveraged him out and took over the company.

"He has been out to ruin me ever since. He's the reason for those guards out there. Thanks to his hired goons from both the Italian and Russian Mafias, there have been several attempts on my life. I've been lucky so far, but there is always a chance my luck will run out. I can't afford to let that happen. I intend to destroy him financially so he cannot afford to hire anyone for anything."

"Why don't you go to the police? You didn't need to become a criminal and murderer yourself?"

His voice grew hard. "Oh, believe me I tried. You see I moved my mother to the villa in Menton and furnished it like a palace. I still remember her face when she walked back into it after all those years. Unfortunately, she did not get to enjoy it for long. Someone tried to burn the villa and they murdered my mother. We assume she was attempting to stop them. The servants called for an ambulance, but my mother bled to death before they arrived. Fortunately, they were able to quickly douse the fire. I suspected Ogden was responsible and told the French police, but they could find no evidence and they never arrested a suspect. That's when I decided he would suffer for my mother's death."

"Suppose he's innocent of that?"

"No. I don't believe it. He hated us too much." She heard him take a deep breath before he continued, "When you call me a murderer, that may be true technically, but I prefer to think of myself as judge and jury. Those two men who brought you on the boat murdered the shopkeeper. They were not innocent altar boys. Both were Italian Mafia working as hired assassins. Was it my place to kill them? No, but under the circumstances, they deserved everything they got. Besides, do you know how I learned about them?"

"Obviously, not."

"They were hired by my former boss to kill me. When they failed, he fired them. I learned who they were and hired them. Do you really need to mourn the loss of two hired killers? Should I be damned for saving the courts a lot of time and money?"

"What about the two that killed them? Who were they?"

"Same story, only they are Russian. They also tried to kill me, failed and were fired. Thanks to my Russian heritage, they readily agreed to work for me."

"I'm surprised you would hire someone who had tried to kill you."

"These are professionals. It is nothing personal to them. It's just a job they do for money…mine or Ogden's…it doesn't matter whose."

Lila leaned back in her chair. She did not know whether to believe him or not. A part of her wanted to, but she kept remembering the kindness one of the men on the boat had shown her. Surely, the one she called Chef was not all bad. "I've heard your story, so let's get on with it. What exactly do you expect me to do?"

"A few years ago, I quit my job as CEO. Not long after that, the stock crashed, and the company was purchased at pennies on the dollar during a leveraged take-over. That suited me fine. Unbeknown to my nemesis, I had gained access to all his account numbers. He had them written on a piece of paper that he had left in the very back of his desk. I leafed through the other papers in the file, but only the account numbers interested me. Apparently, when Ogden vacated the office so I could move in, he forgot the file was there. For whatever reason, I still have the other papers in the file in the villa in Menton. I should have trashed them.

"At any rate, after he was forced out of the company, he went into politics and has fooled enough people to move up in the political ranks. He is now a state senator and using the system to make even more money through selling his influence. I have the numbers for his bank in New York, his offshore bank accounts, and his investment accounts. Unfortunately, I don't have the passwords. That's where you come in. You are going to find them, access those accounts, and then we are going to drain every single one. However, we do nothing until you have the passwords to access all accounts. Then we will hit them all at once."

"And you think I can do that?"

"Mrs. Cord," his voice became very soft, "You had better hope you can. And don't think you can email or contact someone to help you escape, every site you visit will be monitored and the minute you try that, you will no longer be of use to me. Do you understand what I am saying?"

Lila turned and stared at the dark computer screen, refusing to respond to his question. Despite the softness of his tone, there was steel underneath. He would get what he wanted from her, or she suspected she might well be a dead woman. If his story held water, did he just want her to believe that he would kill an innocent woman? Or, was he capable of it if he were obstructed in going after what he wanted? It was a question she would need time to ponder.

"You'll find a dossier on the man inside that folder on the desk. Perhaps, something in it will help you with determining what passwords he might use. If you need any software not already installed on your computer, just speak what you need. My assistant will hear you and will get it installed remotely. Now, why don't you get on with it. The sooner you get me what I want, the sooner you can leave."

Lila neither responded nor turned around. With resignation, she leaned forward and turned on the computer.

Chapter 10

At dawn all three men woke up in a bad mood from a restless night. The first thing Quint did was check the recording on the computer that they had set to monitor the villa. He was frustrated that there had been no light signal. Either Lila did not understand the hidden message in the advertisement on TV, or she was unable to control the light in her room. He dared not consider any other alternatives. Buster and Freddie awakened with headaches from too much wine at dinner the previous evening. They were almost as disappointed as Quint that there had been no signal from Lila. All three sat silently chewing their breakfast and sipping coffee as they stared morosely across the lake. The view was doing nothing to cheer them up. Their pity-party was interrupted by the shrill ringing of the phone. Quint put his cup down and walked to the bedside table.

"Hello."

"I'm sorry to disturb you Mr. Cord. You have a visitor who insists on coming up to see you. I cannot allow this without your permission."

"Of course. Put him on the phone, please." Quint was curious who would be coming to see him at seven in the morning.

"Quint, I'm agent Jimmy Rutherford from the Milan office. Director Williams told me to haul ass up here first thing this morning with some gadgets he thinks will be useful. I need you to tell the desk clerk it is alright for me to come up."

"Yeah, no problem. Put him on the line."

Quint assured the clerk that his visitor was welcome. After Jimmy got the room number, he walked over to the elevator, punched the button and rose to the second floor. In minutes he was knocking on Quint's door.

Quint opened the door and ushered Jimmy in. He introduced him to Buster who came over to shake hands. Before he could introduce Freddy, Jimmy said, "Hey, Freddy-boy, I wondered where the office computer guru had got off to. I should have known you would be here."

Other than a nod of acknowledgement, Freddy did not comment. It was obvious that Freddy didn't like being called Freddy-boy.

Turning back to Quint, Jimmy said, "The Director tells me you need some of our toys. I have some I think you are going to love."

"If you brought the ones I'm thinking of, you're damned right they are." Freddy grinned as he stared at the large box Jimmy had set on the floor.

"Yep, Director Williams requested I bring our latest toys. He glanced at Quint and Buster, "You're not going to believe these little gadgets I have. One looks like a house fly, but it's a drone equipped with a highly sophisticated camera. It even sounds like a fly. We can fly it remotely all over the inside of that damned villa where your wife is being held. Then, there's one a little larger that looks like a bumble bee. It can carry a powerful explosive anywhere you want it. It's also remote controlled, and like the fly, all it takes is an opened door or window to get in. I've even flown them down a chimney. One way or another, we will get in. The third one is our standard aerial surveillance drone with heat sensitive capability. That way we don't have to depend solely on satellite feeds to monitor the villa. I have a van parked outside that is equipped to operate the three drones. We will need to move it to a location that puts the control module within range of the villa."

"How about opening that up and let's see these little gismos?" Buster pointed to the box on the floor. Buster and Quint stood mesmerized as Jimmy lined up the three drones on the table. Picking up the FX9 that looked like a housefly, Jimmy put it on the palm of his left hand and began to point out the features. As he talked, Quint studied the thing. It looked amazingly life like. He could only hope that the villa did not possess a fly swatter. He could not help himself when he asked what if it were swatted.

"That would have to be the fastest and toughest swatter on record. This thing is unbelievable and tough as hell. I'm not worried about that. The one thing we must concern ourselves with is closed doors. I can perch this above a closed door until it is open, give it a quick flight in to check around, and then fly it out the next time the door is opened. Wherever they have your wife, they will have access to her to take her food and so forth, so at some point they will open the door to where she is being held."

Quint nodded as Jimmy explained, and then pointed to the mid-sized that resembled a large bumble bee. "Tell me about this one."

"Right. That one is the BZ20 It's bigger so it's not as innocuous. We don't want to send it in until we have a definite target. I want to find a remote spot and do some test runs to determine the amount of explosive we need for this operation, the detonation time, etc. I suspect we won't be using it until we are ready to execute an extraction."

"Got it. The largest one...the UAV?"

"Yeah. The Spynel Unmanned Aerial Vehicle is equipped

with Infrared technology, weighs in at 20 pounds and has a wingspan of four feet. We can send it high enough to make it unobtrusive and keep it stationery over the site we are monitoring. We'll use it for general surveillance. As I said, it is also equipped with a heat-seeker mode. We will be able to locate all persons in the villa with its technology. I suggest that we go up in the mountains and test out all three. Freddy and I have been trained on the operation of them. You guys are going to be the extraction team; but you need to see how they work, and what we can expect them to do for us in this particular operation."

Buster looked over at Quint. "Should someone stay here while we check these out? I don't feel right about not monitoring the villa."

Quint turned to Freddy who was returning the drones to the box. "Freddy, you already know what these will do and how to operate them. Since you have more computer experience than either Buster or I, would you mind staying behind?"

"That's fine. As a matter of fact, I was going to suggest it. Jimmy, do you have a site in mind? If not, I can make a suggestion."

"Nope. Where do you think we can do this? I don't want anyone nosing around checking out what we are doing, so it needs to be remote."

"Across the lake from Lugano is the town of Melano. There is a road leading from there up to Monte Generoso. Along the way there are some side roads that lead off into pretty wild country. That should provide you what you need for testing these out. Did you bring the usual assortment of explosives?"

"Yeah, C4, some grenades, etc. They're in the van. I'll brief them on the way." He nodded to Quint, "You guys ready to roll?"

Quint said, "Sure. You want to use the john or anything before we get on the road?"

"Nope. I'm good."

Freddy sat at the computer, as the three men left the room. He really hated to miss the demonstrations, but there was a job to be done. When it came to monitoring computer activity originating from the villa, that was where his expertise was most useful. He shook his head. Dammit, he was proud of those toys and loved working with them. He thought he was better at the remotes than Jimmy, as well. However, he knew he had to suck it up, as Jimmy was not much good at the kind of hacking he needed to do.

*****

Jimmy turned onto a small road on the left flank of Monte Generoso that soon petered out into a pile of scree. In minutes, he was showing Buster and Quint what the new toys from the Milano office could do. It wasn't until he loaded the "bumble bee" BZ20 with C4, that both men stood in open mouthed shock when it delivered the load on target and detonated.

"Holy Hell!" Buster exclaimed. "Who would have thought a little thing like that could pack such a wallop."

Jimmy laughed, "I can double the C4 load, but you damned sure don't want to be standing anywhere around here. I can also arm it with a small directional cyanide dart. That gives a trajectory similar to a bullet."

Buster looked at them longingly. "Hell. I'm going to see if Gerald will get these things for my tool bag."

Jimmy shook his head. "You're a private contractor. These are specific government tools and they are as expensive as hell.

There aren't all that many of them even for us to use. Still since you do government work for the Agency, you can try. If that doesn't work, there are some available on the internet but they're nowhere near the quality of these.

Quint encouraged, "Go for it, Buster. I'll second the request. It may work."

Jimmy agreed, "Yeah, you can try."

"I'm as impressed as Buster. However, first things first. The important thing right now is figuring out how to use these gadgets…excuse the pun…to get the most bang for our buck." Quint flexed his jaw as he waited for Jimmy's reply.

"That's your job. I've got the equipment the Agency provided, the van, and both Freddy and I are here to help rescue your wife. But it is on you to figure out how you want it done. If something goes wrong…"

"Yeah, I know. You don't want to take the fall." Quint could not keep the bitterness from his voice. Even in the CIA, there were those who first wanted to cover their asses. Apparently, Jimmy fell into that category.

"Hey, man. Don't go sour on me. We're going to do everything we can to make sure it goes off without a hitch." Jimmy's face wore a chagrined look that Quint ignored.

Buster shook his head at the Milan asset, "Man, if it were your wife that had been kidnapped, I suspect your fuse would be running a little short, too."

Jimmy hid his red face by leaning over and fiddling with the computer controls as he sent the larger drone into the air. The three men stared at the crisp image on the screen as the drone circled the surrounding area. Switching to heat seeking mode, Quint and Buster stared as the three of them were picked up on the computer screen.

After the three devices had been put through various tests, Jimmy led them back to the van where he opened a large locker. Inside were four Heckler and Koch HK416D assault rifles, six Glock 19 pistols, a jumble of CDQ knives, boxes of ammunition, Kevlar vests, six AN/PVS-21 night vision goggles, and four MBITR's.

"Multiband Inter/Intra Team Radio...they'll come in handy." Quint said as he picked one up.

"That's right. Let me show you two how it works."

"No need, Buster and I have used these before."

Buster leaned over and picked up a CDQ knife. He remarked as he held one up, "These knives are the ones the SEALs use. I have several myself. There's nothing I like better for hand to hand combat."

"Yeah, they are mean son-of-a-bitches." Jimmy remarked as he began packing up.

While he reorganized the van, Quint and Buster walked over to a cliff and stared out at the distant town of Lugano nestled on the opposite shore of the lake. Both were lost in their own thoughts. It was now up to them to determine the next step. They had one chance to pull off a rescue. They could not afford any screw-ups.

Jimmy had little to say on the drive back into Lugano and neither did the other two men. Buster and Quint were both pondering ways of going into the villa to rescue Lila. Jimmy was aware of his earlier gaffe and did not want to call attention to himself until the residue of Quint's anger had subsided. He was ambitious and wanted to move up in the CIA ranks. He could not afford to alienate a man that the Director considered a personal friend.

When they returned to the Hotel Splendide, Freddy greeted them at the door, excitement evident in his face. "She's online. At least, I suspect it's her. At any rate, assuming it is, someone tried to log onto a bank account in the States, one in the Bahamas, one in Switzerland, and two investment accounts. I looked up the numbers and was able to trace them back to a senator from California. The only one I couldn't get a read on is the one in Switzerland, but if it fits the pattern, it is probably the same guy. I typed in his name and did some research. You ain't gonna believe his tie to Lyon Owens!" Freddy stopped and looked expectantly at the other three men before continuing. "It seems Lyon worked for this guy, and after working his way up in the man's company, grew some claws and edged him out. From the news articles, that resulted in some bad blood on the Senator's part. I found this French news article that says Owens thought his former boss was responsible for Lyon's mother's murder, but nothing was ever proven, and his allegations were discredited by the press and the local police. It looks to me like there could be a vendetta going on."

Quint screwed up his mouth and stood in deep thought before asking, "Were the accounts broken into? And who is this mystery boss?"

"Not yet that I can tell; but I really don't think so since they keep getting pinged. I'm trying to track keystrokes so I can follow any progress in that direction. Let me get back to that; and while I'm monitoring these accounts, you can fill me in on anything you have new."

"The boss?" Quint asked again.

"Oh yeah, sorry. His name is Nicholas Ogden. After he lost

the position in the company he founded, he moved back to his home state of California. It appears he didn't do much for a couple of years, and then he ran for the state legislature and lost. After that, he began to court some powerful players and ran again. He won one of the senate seats for California and has held it ever since."

Buster asked, "Do you think he's after our boy Lyon, or is it the other way around. As I see it, except for the suspicion about his mother's murder, Lyon should have no axe to grind with the man. After all, he edged him out, took over the company, made a killing selling out, and went on to bigger and better things. Other than the thing in Menton where he accused Ogden of the murder of his mother, there has never been any mention of Lyon trying to finger Ogden, has there? We need to check that."

"That may be true," Quint posited, "but there's a reason Ogden's accounts are under the gun. Of course, it could be sheer coincidence and have nothing to do with Lyon. No doubt Ogden has made some enemies during his political career."

Freddy piped up, "Quint, why don't you do some on-line research and see if you can dig up any dirt that might point to someone else having it in for the senator. I'm going to keep monitoring Ogden's accounts to see if one of them is accessed."

"Sure." Turning to Buster he directed, "Buster…if you will…via the satellite monitor, keep an eye on the guards and any comings or goings from the villa."

Quint paused, "That reminds me, Jimmy, should we move the van and get the drone in position to start monitoring heat signals? It seems to me, if we find an image that stays put in one location, it makes sense that would be Lila…especially since it's doubtful she's had any real freedom to move about. If she did, my girl would be looking for a way out of there."

"No problem, I'll get the van over there, but we can't do an all-nighter without some kind of back-up."

"Freddy, can you spell him? Without more training, I'm not sure how effective Buster and I would be with your fancy drones. I can arrange for some food and anything else you guys need." Quint looked at Freddy for his answer.

"Yeah, I'll cover the night shift until it looks like everyone has settled down for the night...except for the night watch...then I'll come back and get some sleep. And we'll start again in the morning."

"Great. Jimmy, can you cover until 8:30 or so when Freddy comes to relieve you? After that, maybe you can do six-hour shifts. Freddy, can you track Lila from the van?"

"No problem."

"Sounds good. I'll keep in touch via text messages if I pick up on anything unusual." Jimmy left to visit his room before leaving for the first shift in the van.

Freddy turned back to his computer to see if someone was able to access any of Ogden's accounts. Although he could not be sure that Lila was the one trying to hack in, his gut told him it was. As for why Lyon had his claws out for Ogden, he did not have a clue.

Quint was soon busy researching the life history of Senator Nicholas Ogden. He began with current history figuring that any enemies were political ones. On the surface, Ogden appeared be to a do-nothing who enjoyed the status of his office more than the chore of sponsoring laws. Speaking engagements, campaigning and charity balls were about all he could find on the man during his years in the Senate. Frustrated that this exercise was getting him nowhere, he started going through his tenure with his company. Other than being a hard-nosed businessman there seemed to be little of note. Quint nodded in approval when he read that Ogden had helped needy kids get an education and guaranteed them a job upon graduation. Again, nothing rang a bell. Digging further into the man's history, he unearthed an interesting nugget. Shortly after college, one Nikolai Ogneff changed his name to Nicholas Ogden. After further research, Quint found where his parents had immigrated to the US from Russia when Nicholas was a small boy.

Leaning back in his chair, Quint stared out at the water in deep thought. Nothing so far indicated anything nefarious in the man's history, not even the changing of his name to an Americanized version as so many immigrants before him had done. Playing a wild hunch, Quint typed in Lyon Owens name and began to dig. An hour later he found what he was looking for. Owens' father, Lucas Owens married a French woman named Tatiana Karnéev. She was the daughter and only child of Prince Egor Karnéev and his wife Olenka who fled Russia during the revolution and settled at their villa in Menton, France. Both Lyon and Nicholas Ogden were born of Russian parents. Was there some significance in the Russian connection buried somewhere in their life story? If so, was there a vendetta between the two that went beyond Owens take-over of Ogden's company?

Freddy interrupted Quint's musings with a sudden cry. "She's online!"

"Any clue what she's doing?"

"No. It looks like she is using some encrypted program. I have no clue what it is or how to break in."

Quint looked down at his computer and exclaimed, "I can't

believe I can be so stupid. I totally forgot this is Lila's laptop. Hers is better than mine, so we decided just to bring this one and leave mine. She wrote her own hacking program and I lay you odds that's what she's using. There is nothing out there that even comes close to what my girl can do with her little invention."

"Can you use it?"

Before Quint could reply, a message popped on the screen. It was from Lila.

Chapter 11

Lila flipped open the folder the man had left for her and began to read. It contained a detailed life history of Senator Nicholas Ogden of California, formerly CEO of the Caspio Corporation. When she got to the part where Ogden had been edged out by the company CFO there was a gap. The chronology picked up with Ogden's move to California. While she found it odd that there was no mention of the CFO's name or how he maneuvered to edge Ogden out, she could only assume that her captor did not want her to know that information. Although it niggled at the back of her mind, she shrugged her shoulders and began typing in the account numbers and the names of the institutions associated with them. She then set up an automatic notification system that would alert her when one of the accounts was accessed. After that she entered the first of the bank account numbers at the Republic Bank in New York along with Ogden's name and began to try to access it. Using the information in the dossier she tried a couple combinations with no luck. Any further attempts would result in a temporary lock on the account. Guessing at passwords and getting them right in two tries was an exercise in wasted time and there was too great a chance that anyone monitoring these accounts would be tipped off by the attempted accesses. What she needed was some good up to date hacking software that was web silent as those provided on his computer were worthless. She thought for several minutes of the various programs she knew and had used. The best was probably the one she herself had developed and used when she tracked the North Korean several months back. The idea of sharing it was anathema to her, but she had no choice. Besides, she knew how to remove it without anyone knowing she had done so. Once she had done as her captor directed and drained Ogden's accounts, she would make sure it was deleted.

Turning towards the mirror, she asked, "I'm going to download a hacking program from my personal computer. I will be using an access code that will allow me to get in even if it is turned off. Is that a problem?"

"No. Just don't try to contact anyone." The man's voice that answered her was high pitched with a trace of an accent, unlike the more sonorous voice of her captor.

"I should have it soon and will download it to your computer so you can follow what I am doing."

"I do not know of this program or I would already have obtained it."

"You don't know it because the program is one that I developed." Lila wondered if she could soften the guy up and induce some sympathy. She smiled at the mirror, "Since we are both computer nerds, we should be friends. Do you have a name? Mine's Lila, Lila Cord."

"Yes, I know who you are. The boss does not allow us to use any names with you. This is for your safety as well as ours."

"Of course." Lila arose from the desk and started exploring her room and the attached bath. She was amazed anew at the thoroughness of the preparations made for her. But her main emotion was not amazement, but rather, simple glee. With her program, she would outsmart them and let Quint know where she was being held. All it would take would be a temporary block of the assistant so he would not know who she accessed.

She would explain it as a glitch in the program that rarely happened, and one she was still trying to correct. If she could but let her husband know where she was being held, he would move heaven and earth to set her free. She could not restrain the smile that suffused her face as she looked at her reflection in the bathroom mirror. At least she knew that it was not a one-way window as a medicine cabinet stocked with aspirin, band aids and other assorted basics was behind it. Closing the toilet lid, she sat while she waited for the assistant to download her program. It felt good to be away from prying eyes for those few minutes.

It was not long before she heard his voice on the speaker in the other room letting her know that the program was downloaded and ready for her to use. Standing up, she squared her shoulders and returned to the computer.

The first order of business was to download the account numbers and set up an alert to tell her the moment anyone tried to log on to an account. She would then be able to track their keystrokes to capture the access code. Once she had those, her captor could do what he damned well pleased to the accounts. Despite feeling some sympathy for him after hearing his life story, she could not condone the actions of a man that would kill without remorse, kidnap at will, and then force her to steal the life's savings of another man...even if he were as evil as the captor presented.

Lila did not know where she was being held, but she now had the name of the person her captor was going after. With that information, perhaps Quint would find her captor's name in the man's history and could use that to find where he was holding her. She could describe the room she was in, but with no clue where it was located within the villa, she wasn't sure of what use that would be. Her message would have to be transmitted quickly, one quick bit of vital information to keep from triggering an alarm with her human watchdog. Logging into her program, she deliberately triggered the erase keystrokes setting and another setting that hid her on-line status. He would only see her typing if he looked through the mirror. Hopefully, he would assume that she was setting up the program to track Ogden's accounts, and he would not be suspicious.

"Held captive crack financial accts Sen. Ogden. I think large villa. Where? Unharmed. Find me please. Love L." Lila hit send and prayed.

In seconds, the assistant's voice demanded, "What are you up to? I am supposed to follow everything you're doing."

Lila put her hands in her lap and held them to stop shaking, "It's ok-k-kay." Damn. Stuttering made her sound guilty as held.

Making a concerted effort at control, she continued, "Hey, I'm just trying to get the program set up so I can tie you in and start entering the account numbers. It doesn't just open like a normal app. I have it encrypted. You have to give me a second if you want it shared with you while I work."

"Make it quick. You do anything stupid, and it is not just your neck in the wringer; mine is, too."

"Cool it. Do you think I don't know that? I'm trying my best to do what's expected so I can get out of here."

"Get on with it. The sooner the better. I don't like playing watchdog."

Lila bit back a smart reply. She could not afford to antagonize the man. Resting her fingers on the keyboard, she activated tracking for the assistant and began to enter the correct protocol to set up the hacking program to get into the accounts. Once the numbers were all entered, she coded them to alert her the minute someone tried to log into one of them. At that point, she would capture the password and record that for the time that the captor wanted the funds transferred. For her it was easier than tracking the wily North Korean who knew how to hide his IP address, constantly morph to new ones, and route his online activities through various sites to camouflage his location. Banking and investment accounts when she already had the account numbers were a piece of cake for her to hack into compared to the wily Korean.

Once the account numbers were entered, it was a waiting game to see if one of them would be accessed. At that point she would grab the password, and the account would be open to her to do whatever her captor ordered. Glancing at the clock on the wall, and judging by the hollow feeling in her stomach, the woman should be bringing her a meal shortly. In the meantime, Lila leaned back in the chair. She thought about trying to start a conversation with the assistant but decided that was pointless. Standing up, Lila walked to the bathroom and closed the door. While she was in there, the assistant activated the microphone to order her to stay there until the woman bringing her meal could leave. Again, Lila closed the toilet lid and waited. At least the food was beyond just good. Five minutes later she was told she could come out. Lila walked over to the desk where a tray was waiting by the computer. A delicate Sole Meunière, a fresh green mixed salad, and delicate and crispy truffled fries were accompanied by a half bottle of Pouilly-Fuissé. A delicate Pommes Anna completed the meal. Lila smiled. Once again, the food was perfect.

She could not resist tweaking the assistant, "Since I am such a special guest, I bet the hired help doesn't eat nearly as well."

She waited to see if he would answer. She had already begun eating the perfectly cooked fish when he responded.

"Mr. O..." He quickly stopped himself when he realized he had almost said his employer's name. He could only hope the man was not listening. Continuing, he said, "You would be wrong, the boss has a wonderful chef. We all get to enjoy the same meals you are having. Please, just shut up and eat. We don't need to speak of anything except what we have been assigned to do."

"I am sorry. You are right of course." Lila smiled; she would now think of her captor as Mr. O.

Lila finished her meal and was contemplating opening the Murphy Bed to test it for comfort, when her computer alerted her that one of the accounts was being accessed. It was the one in Switzerland. Sitting up in her chair, she quickly established the tracking protocol and began waiting for the password to pop up on her screen. Hurriedly she wrote it down. Next, she would know why the account was being accessed. The minute the log-off screen popped up to signal the end of the transaction, Lila logged back into the account and went to the menu. There she clicked on recent transactions and jotted down the information. Mr. O might not be interested, but she was curious. The activity log showed that one hundred thousand dollars had been transferred to AFGU at an account in the Caymans. She had never heard of it, but it was something she could look up later if Mr. O needed her to do so. Another fifty thousand had been transferred to a Swiss account under the name of Rolf Schmidt.

The assistant spoke, "I have it. I'll let the boss know we are into the Swiss account."

Lila logged out of the account and resumed her wait to see if another account would be accessed. After an hour of nothing else happening, Lila stood and stretched. Grabbing a nightgown and robe she went to the bathroom to prepare for bed. Coming out, she pulled down the Murphy bed and was pleased to see top quality linens on what looked to be an invitingly comfortable bed. She was folding back the covers to climb in when Mr. O's voice came over the intercom.

Owens was puzzled at the transfer of such a large sum to AGFU. Something about that niggled at his memory but he could not identify why that should be so. The other matter was a greater priority. "Good job. I want you to delay your bedtime long enough to go into the Schmidt account and block it so he cannot access those funds. The man is a hired assassin, no doubt being paid to come after me. I need to stall that if I can in order to beef up security here. When he tries to get into his account and cannot, he will be furious. Hopefully, he will think Ogden is responsible. Can you block him?"

"That's simple. I have his account number at the Swiss bank. All I need to do is enter it and put in enough invalid passwords that the bank will freeze the account. If he is notified and tries to set up a new password, I can capture it and withdrawn his funds. Where do you want me to send them?"

Mr. O chuckled. "Send them to your own account if you like. Think of it as payment for saving me from another attempt on my life. That seems like poetic justice to me."

"Thank you, but I don't think so." Lila did not want anyone backtracking an illegal transfer to her.

"Ah, such scruples." He chuckled again, "Very well, use this account. Are you ready to write?"

"Just a minute." Lila sat down at the desk and picked up her pen. "Ready."

Moments later the Schmidt account was frozen. Setting up an alert on the account number, she decided to try to get some rest.

Lila lay in bed unable to sleep. She kept thinking how easy it was to access the first account. If Ogden soon accessed the others, she could be released. At least, she hoped Mr. O would live up to the promise to set her free once she had done what he asked. The only problem was not knowing how frequently the Senator logged into the different accounts. She could be sitting for weeks waiting for him to go into the investment portfolio. The idea of being penned up in a windowless room for weeks waiting for a computer alert on one of the accounts was her idea of utter boredom. But what else could she do? She was a prisoner just as much as someone in jail. The only difference was the degree of comfort and the quality of the food. With not even a book or a television for diversion and with her time on the computer restricted to what he wanted from her, there was nothing to do but eat, sleep, and wait. After an hour of endless circling around the same thoughts, Lila thumped her pillow, rolled on to her side and soon fell into a restless sleep.

The next morning, she was showered, dressed, and waiting when her breakfast was delivered. Again, she had to wait in the bathroom until the woman put the tray down and left. After Lila finished her breakfast, she stood up and began to pace the room, counting steps as she did so. Mr. O's voice came on when she had counted to 369 steps. She stopped and turned toward the one-way window.

"Good morning, Mrs. Cord. I trust you slept well?"

"Not very."

"I realize you are a bit restless and bored, judging from the pacing. You understand, I cannot permit you to leave the room not knowing when one of the accounts will be accessed; however, if you will tell me the kind of books you enjoy, I will arrange to have some delivered to you. Also, I will have a small television installed. That is the best I can do."

Lila listed some books that she had been meaning to read but had not gotten around to. She also asked for some magazines. When asked for a tourist guide to the local area, he laughed.

"Mrs. Cord, you are clever. For the moment, you don't need to know where you are. If all goes well, I will see to it that you get a guidebook when you are released."

"You can't blame me for trying." Lila grinned despite herself. "The books and television would be a big help."

"Yes, I'm sure. As for the television, it will only access movie channels so there will be no programming local or otherwise."

"But, of course there won't." Lila shrugged. Mr. O was thorough if nothing else.

The next hour found her pacing again as she waited for an alert. Just when she had given up on one of the accounts being accessed that morning, the computer sounded an alert.

It was the Schmidt account. Lila's fingers were poised on the keyboard ready to capture the password the second it was entered. Minutes later nothing more had happened. Lila started at the screen in puzzlement. He should have already logged on. After five minutes more, Lila typed in Schmidt's account number. Immediately a screen popped up saying the account had been closed. Lila swore steadily under her breath. In moments the assistant's voice came over the microphone.

"What happened?"

"I can only guess that he was alerted by the bank that someone was trying to break into the account. He must have gone to the bank and either withdrawn the money or switched it to a new account bypassing log-in protocol."

"Do you know the location of the bank?"

"Give me a few minutes and I can find it."

Five minutes later, Lila announced, "The bank is in Zurich."

"I'll let the boss know what is going on. He's going to be extremely pissed."

"Hey, don't blame me."

"You did screw up by entering too many wrong passwords, so online access was blocked."

"Look, I did exactly what I was told to do by your boss. You heard him tell me. I'm trying all I know to do to get him what he wants so I can get out of here"

He snarled, "See that you do. Otherwise, you are a waste of time."

Lila was just bored and angry enough to snap, "You do realize that we are both working for the same guy. You don't need to be so nasty. I am doing everything asked of me. Believe me, I want out of here as badly as you must want me gone. What's the deal with you? Does it offend your male ego that he wanted me on this job instead of you?"

Unbeknown to either of them, Mr. O was listening. When he came back on the microphone, she had no idea, but he obviously had heard the last exchange. "You are both acting like brats. Stop bickering. I am going to tell you what we will be doing next. So, simmer down and listen. If his hired muscle attacks, it won't just be my life on the line."

Lila thought to herself, oh wonderful, as if things aren't bad enough already.

Chapter 12

Quint grinned to himself. Now that he knew Lila was safe and he had the means to extract her, it was merely a matter of sending in the drones to determine her location within the villa and then formulate a rescue plan. He was so bemused by his thoughts he did not hear when Freddy spoke to him.

"Hey, Quint. This is one hell of a program your wife developed. I just saw her pick up on one of Ogden's accounts, the one in Switzerland. Ogden just transferred funds from his Swiss bank in Zurich to some Rolf Schmidt guy and to AFGU. You ever heard of AFGU?"

"Nah, you?"

"Nope. Why don't you run AFGU down? I'll try to get the low down on this Schmidt guy. It would be interesting to know why the good senator is sending this kind of money to third parties."

"I'm on it." Quint immediately typed in AFGU and started digging.

The letters stood for the Alliance for Global Union. The more he dug the more alarmed for the Western World he became. Buried under several layers of protection, Quint found the list of their objectives.

The first was the creation of a Global Union with existing countries reduced to the role of dependent states. Schools would be mandated to inculcate the basic tenets of the new Nation in all children: reduced patriotism to existing Countries, elimination of all positive aspects of a Country's history with a new concentration on the negative, a prohibition of National Anthems, patriotic songs, and National pledges, the promotion of clubs with the theme of a united world with music and other activities around that idea. Religions would be slowly eliminated to be replaced by a belief in the primacy of man and the ideal of a universal brotherhood of equality in all aspects of life. By doing these things, tribalism and devotion to one's ancestors and country would be eliminated.

By first uniting the Western World in the Global Union with all armies and assets under its control, the Global Union would then subjugate all other countries that might resist the coming world order. All private firearms would be confiscated with resistors subjected to the death penalty. Mandatory adult training sessions would promulgate the canons of the new Union: to provide free health care at all stages of life, to make abortion easily available at any stage of pregnancy, to encourage euthanasia among the ill and elderly population as a patriotic ideal, to levy taxes sufficient to eliminate income inequality, and to enact a law stipulating that at death all estates would become the property of the Union. Finally, all businesses and economic activity would exist under heavy government monitoring and controls. Pods would be created under a leader to monitor all persons living in each local area with strict reporting of any infractions or resistance to the new ideals. An independent media would be eliminated and replaced by government-controlled news agencies that reported only the news sanctioned by the Global Union.

The more Quint read, the more disgusted he became. Next, he clicked on the funding sources and leaders of the movement. Here things became murky.

Leaning back in his chair, he stared at the lake. The water had darkened with the clouds rolling in to signal an approaching storm. After a moment, he said, "Buster, Freddy, I need you to listen to this and tell me what you think is going on and how this ties in."

Quint proceeded to tell them of the AFGU organization and its objectives. Both men listened with growing concern. When he had finished, he asked, "The question is why is a United States Senator contributing to this organization? Is he a part of it? Who else is involved in this cabal?"

Freddy asked, "Did you look for a Board of Directors, Officers' names?"

"Yeah, but I can't access that. The only thing I could get into is what I just read to you."

Buster exclaimed, "Dammit, what in the hell is going on and how do this Owens guy and Lila tie into it? Or is it just a coincidence?"

"That I don't know." Quint shrugged his shoulders. Things were becoming more complicated by the moment, and he didn't like it one bit.

"Let's get some dinner sent up because I'm going to have to relieve Jimmy soon. So far, the only thing that I can get from tracking Lila is she entered enough false passwords to lock the account of this Schmidt guy," Freddy remarked.

Quint turned to Buster, "You picking up on anything new at the villa?

"It looks like more of those Rottweilers have been let loose on the grounds. And the guards aren't doing the normal rotation. Owens must have put them on an alert."

"You don't think he's on to us, do you?" Quint was terrified that Owens had picked up on their presence and was adding an additional layer of security. It was difficult enough as it was; more dogs and a more rigorous guard schedule just made it tougher. "Freddy, get in touch with Jimmy and see if he was able to get one of those drones into the villa."

"Give me a minute and I'll log into his computer. If he got a drone in, we'll be able to see wherever the drone went. Quint, I'm going to log you and Buster into the coordinates for the infrared images. You watch that for me and document any location that appears to have a stationary body. At the moment, we're not worried about those people that are moving around. The first objective is to determine where Lila is being held. Once we figure that out, then we see if there is a pattern to the other human locations."

"Can you tell if they are male or female on these images?" Quint asked.

"Sometimes the body size or shape will give you a clue. But you can't always count on that since someone who is really thin or obese is difficult to determine by just heat signature." Freddy typed for a moment while Quint and Buster waited to see if he could learn anything.

Buster looked over at Quint, "You doing okay, pal?"

"Yeah. I'm hanging on. Not much else I can do until we can figure out how to get Lila out of there."

Buster nodded his head in sympathy. He realized from the time that he had known Quint, that the man was not one who opened up easily. Perhaps, it was the result of a childhood where he never felt quite sure of his father's affection. While Quint probably realized his mother loved him, she had never had the backbone to stand up to the stern Mr. Cord. Quint had kept romantic interests to the shallowest of terms until he met and fell for Lila. It was only after a considerable reluctance and her slow recovery from an auto accident that Quint had allowed himself to fall in love with her. Although Quint tried to appear stoic, Buster suspected that underneath the façade the man was in considerable angst. Buster figured that was the reason he had never allowed a woman to get beneath his own skin.

In the work he was in he could not afford the complication and additional worry. Besides, few women would tolerate weeks of non-communication and no explanation for where he had been and what he was doing. For a while, when he first learned that Quint and Lila were marrying, he had been jealous of the intimacy and love that he also wanted deep down. Instead, he continued on the path of casual sexual encounters with women that he seduced and left without looking back.

Tired of endlessly staring at the grounds of the villa, Buster stood up and stretched. "Damn. This gets old. Freddy have you logged onto Jimmy's computer yet?"

"It takes a minute to download, but I'll have it shortly. It takes major protocol each time I log in remote from the main console in the van. That's a security measure in case a laptop gets compromised."

"What happens if someone takes the van and tries to use the drone controls?" Quint was curious.

"It automatically shuts down if you don't use the proper access routine," Freddy replied. "I'm on if you want to come over here and see what our 'fly'...the FX9 is up to. Damn, I do love that little thing!"

The three men watched as the tiny drone entered a side door when a guard came out. Buzzing in, the 'fly' began to reconnoiter the interior of the villa. As best they could tell it had entered a back hallway with two doors opening into other areas. As the FX9 circled, they could see into a kitchen, with a cook and what they took to be an assistant, and what appeared to be a pantry area. Ignoring that, the drone continued down the hall through another door that stood slightly ajar. Immediately they were in more opulent surroundings. This was the main foyer of the house. On the left of the front entry door was an elegant salon in the Belle Epoque style with gold gilded cornices and heavy drapery in a white and gold damask. Chairs in Louis XIV style and upholstery in gold and cream stripes flanked a sofa covered in a gold background fabric printed with cream fleur de lis. Paintings in heavy gold frames, Chinese vases, various objets d'arte, and a richly hued oriental carpet attested to the wealth and taste of the owner.

"Sure ain't shabby. This Owens guy has some serious cash!" Buster exclaimed.

The dining room and library were equally impressive as was the master bedroom. After taking a tour of the open areas that allowed access, the little fly-like drone perched on the chandelier in the main hall and waited for one of the closed doors to open. It wasn't long before the kitchen assistant emerged from the back hall carrying a tray laden with food. She knocked on the closed door and was immediately admitted. The fly made a quick surveillance of the room, noting a computer and bed. The man that had opened the door was of medium height with blond hair and a beard. He appeared to be in his late twenties. As the maid exited the room, the drone flew out ahead of her. Hearing the buzz, she swatted at what she thought was a fly. She missed. The drone immediately flew back up to the chandelier and waited for another of the closed doors to open.

Five minutes later, the woman returned to the front hall carrying a second tray. She placed the tray on the floor, knocked, said something, and waited. Instead of the occupant opening the door as the man had done, this time the maid extracted a key from her pocket and opened the door. Again, the drone, entered with her. There was no one in the room that the men could see. The only sign of an occupant was an unmade bed that dropped down from a recessed wall cabinet. The room was furnished like the last one with an array of computer equipment. On one wall was a large mirror, across from that was another closed door. The maid placed the tray on the desk beside the computer and walked over to the closed door where she knocked and said something. Walking back to the entry door, she extracted the key from her pocket. The drone buzzed out just ahead of her. Judging by the expression on her face, the idea of a fly in the house annoyed her. Once more she swatted at it and missed. Darting out the door, the drone resumed its perch on the chandelier as she relocked the door to the room.

"That's it!" Quint's excitement was apparent. "That's where they have Lila. Now, we just must figure out a way to get in there and extract her. Will Jimmy fly the FX9 out, or leave it?"

Freddy replied, "I suspect he will leave it just to keep an eye on that door. I agree with you; that's probably where they have Lila. Locked door, computer, bed…it makes sense."

Buster remarked, "I wonder where this Owens guy is. Can you pull up the drone that is circling the villa and see what the heat seeker is showing us? We know two people are in those office-like rooms with closed doors. One appears to be the room where they are holding Lila. We know there are two women who work in the kitchen. The guy either has added guards or has extended the duty time for the ones he has. We need a count of those men, where they are sleeping and where they are when they are off duty. It would be helpful if you would ask Jimmy to document that for us."

"It's time for me to take the next rotation, so I'll take care of it myself." Freddy beckoned the two men over and gave instructions for monitoring the drones from his laptop until Jimmy returned and could take over.

"I'm going to get us a rough layout of the inside of that villa, and I know just who to ask. I'll check to see if Rosa Magnani is working in the dining room tonight. If she is, I'll have her draw me a rough sketch of the rooms and where the servants sleep. I'll also see if she can give me a count on the guards, what kind of watch they do, and where they sleep. Anything she can tell us about the villa could be vital to our plans."

"She's that taxi driver's sister you told me about?" Buster asked.

"Bingo."

Chapter 13

Lila stared at the computer screen, but it might as well have been blank. Mr. O had just detailed instructions to them if the villa were to be attacked by the latest hired assassin or assassins. Would they all be in danger, or would the assassins be out to eliminate Mr. O and leave the rest of them alone? He had given no clue as to what danger she might be in. Whatever the case, she was going to be locked in regardless…and there was no other escape route besides that locked entry door. The surly assistant had listened as intently as she and asked no questions. His job was to station himself in the foyer with a semi-automatic rifle and a revolver where he would join Mr. O and one of the guards. At least, if he were in the foyer, she could send an email to Quint without anyone knowing. Mr. O appeared to think the Schmidt guy would be coming for him within the next day or two. That's all she knew, and it wasn't nearly enough to provide any comfort. In the meantime, all she could do was wait.

Lila shook her head in resignation and refocused on the computer screen to continue monitoring the accounts. After an hour of tense boredom, she stood and stretched. Turning to the mirror through which the assistant could watch her, she said, "I'm taking a break. If any of the accounts are accessed, the program I installed will alert me."

A noncommittal grunt was the only response. Lila shrugged and walked into the bathroom, closing the door with a resounding bang. Closing the toilet lid, she sat down and studied her nails. She wondered how long it would be before she could get a manicure. The polish that had looked so fresh for her honeymoon, was beginning to grow out leaving an unsightly edge at the base of the nail. That was the least of her worries. The boredom was crushing, but the worst was not knowing what was happening beyond that door that could affect her very life: would the villa be attacked placing her in danger from some assassin; would her captor let her go free or kill her when he was finished with her, and finally; where was Quint and what was he doing to free her? At the thought of her new husband, tears began to leak from the corners of her eyes and trace a path down her cheek. Forcing herself to stand, she stood up and stripped her clothes. Stepping into the shower, she turned the water to full blast. As it beat against her, she could feel the tension draining from her body. She could imagine it swirling down the drain and racing into some stream somewhere…far freer than she. Lila shampooed her hair, then rinsed off the conditioner that had also been provided. When she had toweled off, she put on the gown and robe hanging on the hook behind the door.

Stewing was getting her nowhere. She did not have the books or television that Mr. O had promised. No doubt, his priorities now did not extend to the mundane matter of her idle amusements. Flipping back the covers of the bed she had not bothered to straighten or store, she got in and leaned over to turn off the light on the bedside table. A dim glow lit the room from the various electronic equipment. Rolling on her side to face away from the light, she fluffed her pillow and nestled down. Maybe in some pleasant dream, she would find freedom. There were no dreams that night, only a sound sleep…the first since she had been kidnapped.

She awakened in the morning refreshed and surprisingly

lighthearted. Surely, Mr. O was being unnecessarily an alarmist. There was no way to know if the money sent to Schmidt was for a hit job on her captor. It could be anyone, no one, or related to nothing that entailed a killing. Lila stretched as she got out of bed, touched her toes a couple of times, and swung her torso from side to side. Remaking her bed, she then used the remote to lift it back into place. That done, she went to the bathroom for her morning ablutions. The intercom came on while she was dressing to inform her that her breakfast was arriving and to stay in the bathroom until signaled to leave. Even that reminder of her captivity was not unduly onerous.

Far worse was no sunlight, no way to pass the time, except on a dedicated computer that she could only use to intercept account log-ins. She refused to let herself dwell on factors she could not control. It was a matter of the patient marking of time…time to access the accounts and time for Quint to find and rescue her. If she wanted to survive this ordeal, she needed to keep her wits about her. At some point, she might have to find a way to save herself if no outside rescue came in time. She could not do that unless she stayed focused and alert to all circumstances.

After Lila had eaten her breakfast and had resumed her restless pacing, her thoughts were interrupted by the alert signal from the computer. Hastily she seated herself before the screen and waited to see which one of the accounts was being accessed. She gaped in amazement when all the Senator's account numbers appeared simultaneously on the screen and then immediately vanished. Typing frantically, she began trying to track what was happening to the accounts. Each account she tried to access returned a screen saying account closed.

"Damn," she swore. "Hey, Mr. Assistant, better tell your boss we have a real mess here."

"What are you talking about?

"Just get him. I'm trying to figure it out and I'll tell you both at the same time." Lila decided to try hacking into the Swiss bank where the money transferred had originated and go through their data base to see if she could find the transfer of funds from the original account to a new one. Before she could implement the plan, Mr. O's voice sounded over the intercom. "What seems to be the problem?"

"For some reason, it appears that the senator has either transferred funds into a new account at each of the sites we have identified, or these agencies have implemented a block of some type. Every account number popped up at the same time and when I try to access them, they all show the account closed."

"So, what can you do?"

"I can try hacking into each bank or investment firm and track any recent transactions. It won't be easy as these people have some of the best internet protection in the world for obvious reasons."

"But you can do it?"

"I can try, but I can't promise."

There was a long pause before he responded, "I see. I do hope you live up to your reputation, Mrs. Cord. I am determined to drain the senator's money accounts dry. I'm equally determined, you are going to help me do it. Now, get on with it. The minute you have something, I want to know."

Knowing he was watching, Lila nodded her head and turned back to the computer. Perhaps, the easiest one to hack was not a bank or investment firm, but the senator himself. He could not have been in all those locations at the same time, so it stood to reason he used a computer to log into his accounts. She began by searching his website for an email address at his office. Finding that, she used it to start looking for a domain name that was similar. She figured the address for his senatorial office was not one that he would use for transacting personal business, but it might give her a clue to how his personal account was listed.

*****

Thousands of miles away, the senator was worried. Schmidt had phoned to alert him that someone had hacked into his account. The minute Ogden hung up, he logged into his accounts and immediately transferred his funds into new accounts. He realized years before that he had forgotten some of his private papers when he vacated his corporate office at Caspio. He still cursed himself that in those papers were all his financial account numbers and the location for those accounts. When none of the accounts had ever been tampered with, he had left them alone as not worth the trouble to change as no one knew his passwords. That bothered him; however, what caused nightmares was the other file that he had left behind. It was a copy he had made of the one safely locked in his home safe. He could no longer remember why he had made the copy, but he had…and he had left it. The question that tormented him was whether Owens had found it and realized the importance of it.

For that reason alone, the man could not be allowed to live. He had paid only for the burning of the villa in Menton. The death of Owens' mother was the unfortunate consequence of her attempt to stop the arsonists. He figured if Owens realized the importance of what he had taken, he would have stored it in his old home in Menton. Unfortunately, his goons had set the fire improperly and before they could redo it, Owens' mother had discovered them. Without thinking, one of the thugs had shot her, raising an immediate alarm in the house when the servants began to scream. They had fled without accomplishing their goal. When Owens had triggered an investigation into him, he had abandoned plans to burn the villa in favor of eliminating the man himself.

That file was out there somewhere. He could protect his accounts, but if the secrets in the file he had left behind were exposed, the very foundations of the world would be shaken. Not only would his life be in danger, but the lives of many prominent people both in and out of governments around the globe would be ruined. He dared tell none of them what he had done. His life would be forfeited were he to do so. His only hope was to destroy Owens and everything he owned. Until then, he was not safe. Everything he and others had spent years slowly building toward would be destroyed. He shook his head with resignation. The fools of the world did not realize what AGFU could mean in terms of world peace and prosperity. Tribalistic fervor, devotion to the status quo of nationhood had to end, or there would never be peace. For him, it was a holy cause...one to which he had pledged to work ceaselessly to help implement. It was the only reason he had gone into politics where he could more easily proselytize his vision.

This time Schmidt had better get it right.

* * * * *

After three hours of tedious searching, Lila got lucky. While she was still checking activity on his office email, a new message popped up. It was so obvious, she kicked herself for not guessing it straight away. He was old school at home with the address SenOgden@aol.com. Obviously, the man was proud of his political caché. Immediately she triggered her software to pick up any logins from that IP address and capture the keystrokes. Now all she would have to do was wait. Once in, she would comb his email history for all financial transactions over the last two days.

Walking over to the two-way mirror, Lila announced, "I am locked onto his personal computer. The minute he logs on, my program will capture his keystrokes when he types in his password. Once I have that, I can go through his recent financial transactions and track the money transfers."

Her comment was met with silence. That had never happened before as he was expressly ordered to monitor her at every moment. Although she suspected that sounds from the exterior of her room were muted by some type of barrier, he had always answered. Worried, she rapped on the mirror,

Hey, did you hear me? Are you there? What's going on?"

Nothing. Lila hurried back to the computer and hastily typed out a message to Quint. 'I love you. Don't know what's up, but think villa is being attacked. If you know where I am, please come fast. Lila"

She stood up and looked around her prison. Where could she hide. There was the room she was in and the bathroom. Neither offered any security were someone to break in. Refusing to admit defeat she began exploring the space. Nothing suggested a hiding place until she spotted the bed. If she figured accurately, the length of the bed was shorter than the closet that enclosed it. Were it closed, there should be a gap at the top of the mattress foot of about six feet by two or three feet. Activating the electronic control, Lila closed the bed and watched the doors snap shut. Walking closer she knelt and tried to pull the doors free from the bottom. They didn't move. The space between the doors and along the top edge were too narrow to allow her fingers to get a grip. If she could not, she figured no one else could either.

It appeared to her this was the best hiding place available. Making a snap decision, she lay parallel to the foot of the mattress and pressed the close button on the remote. Quickly she hooked her right arm and leg over the end of the mattress to keep from rolling down as the bed ascended. When it was almost vertical, she rolled onto the bottom edge of the mattress foot as the exterior doors snapped shut. She heard something fall at that moment but ignored it.

In minutes she began to perspire, both as a result of adrenaline pumping into her body and her body heat being trapped in the space. With the enclosure nearly air-tight, she could only pray that her air supply would last if she needed to stay hidden. She had done all she knew to do to save herself. There was nothing more she could do but wait for whatever was going to happen.

It was another five minutes before she realized the noise she had heard was the remote dropping. In a panic, Lila pushed her left arm between the wall and the top of the mattress. Frantically she struggled to search in the tightly confined space. At last her fingers touched the edge of what had to be the control. Every time she tried to grasp hold and pull it up, it slipped from her fingers. Unless she could get it, she was at the mercy of someone to break through and rescue her…or kill her if she called out.

Chapter 14

When Quint returned from his interview with Rosa, he carried in his right hand a rough sketch of the villa's interior. When he entered the room, he glanced over at Buster who suddenly sat straight up in his chair and exclaimed, "What in the hell is that?"

Quint was instantly at his side, "What's going on?"

"Take a look at the feed from the drone over the villa. It sure as heck looks like someone is trying to come over the wall into the grounds."

As they watched, the guards and the dogs rushed to the site where someone was attempting penetration. In moments, three guards were down and all the dogs.

"Holy hell! Who is going after Owens? We know it's not our side…so who?"

Quint groaned, "Oh, my God, what about Lila. Come on, we're hauling ass over there as quickly as we can. Call Freddy and see what they are picking up and tell them to get the BZ20 drone into the air and armed. That may be our only hope until we can get there. I'm going to grab our gear. You put our Glocks into the duffle bag, right?"

"I did, and back up ammo, as well. Let's roll. I'll call Freddy on the way downstairs. You get us a taxi."

"If Jimmy has left, tell him to get the hell back to the villa. We're going to need everyone we can get to help us."

"On it."

Both men raced from the room, Quint with the duffle bag

slung over his shoulder and Buster on the phone.

Behind him, Quint heard Buster growl, "Come on, dammit. Answer the phone."

By the time they reached the foyer, Buster was talking to Freddy, "What the hell is going on? We just caught the drone feed and are on our way. Is Jimmy there?"

"Yeah, he was getting ready to leave when we saw these guys attack the villa. He's staying in case we need to go in before you can get here."

"We are on the way. Where did you park the van?"

Freddy replied with the van location, and Buster responded, "Got it. We will be there ASAP. Unpack the weapons and radios. We're going to need them. Until we get there, just hang on; and get that BZ20 in action until we can arrive with more fire power. When we go in, we'll need Jimmy with us. Can you monitor the BZ20, FX9, as well as the aerial surveillance drone that's circling the villa without him?"

"I'm on it."

"Right," Buster replied to Freddy's response. "Tell Jimmy to get inside the villa grounds with as much firepower as he can haul. Let's hope the remaining guards are too busy fighting to try to stop him if he's spotted."

Quint listened as Buster replied, "Okay, y'all hang in there. Quint just got us a ride. We're on the way. I'll fill him in on what's going down. I don't need to tell you to be careful."

Buster dove into the cab on Quint's heels. Tires were squealing before his door closed. Quint introduced the driver to Buster as they rocketed down the street, "I got lucky. Our driver, Guiseppe Magnani, is the one I told you about. He knows the villa and promises to get us there as fast as humanely possible."

"Nice to meet you, Guiseppe. Anybody who can drive like you has nerve. We're going up against some seriously bad men. By the way, we have some extra weapons. You interested in going commando with the CIA?"

Turning, Quint stared at Buster with his mouth agape. Snapping it shut, he warned, "Hey, Buster, we don't want to get him caught up in something as potentially dangerous as this."

"Tell me what happen at villa. I help. Sound like fun. I like movie about CIA…bad ass, right? I know how shoot good. I in army for three years. Get award for shoot good. How you say it: 'let roll'?"

"It's 'let's roll.'" Quint struggled with indecision, "Man, you think about it. We're going to be up against some mean dudes. Somebody could get killed. We are with the US government, but you're not. I don't want to get you into trouble with the Swiss government. We could use your help, but I don't know how this is going to go down. You could be killed. Hell, we all could."

"Like you just say, let's roll. I shoot. You tell me what do."

Buster reached over the seat and patted his shoulder, "Good man!"

In the back seat, Buster and Quint held on tightly to the door handles as they swerved around curves and other traffic at breakneck speed. Between them, they filled Guiseppe in on the situation beginning with Lila's abduction. Never taking his eyes from the road, he nodded in understanding as he heard the tale unwind.

Quicker than Quint thought possible, they pulled in behind the van. Grabbing the duffle with the weapons, Quint got out of the car. From the direction of the villa he could hear weapon fire. Buster and Guiseppe followed him to the van. Quint tapped once, called out, and quickly entered with the other two on his heels.

Freddy looked up, "Thank God, you're here. Jimmy is hunkered down in some bushes on the side of the villa where there is a terrace door, but without backup, he is afraid to take on that bunch of goons in there. I count five in the attacking force, two at the front, two at the back, and one at the side terrace door close to Jimmy. They are armed with some major shit. We have the weapons Jimmy showed you. I just hope they're enough."

"No sweat, you have a small arsenal in the van, plus we have our own Glocks. First off, is anyone in the villa giving return fire."

"Yeah, but it is nowhere as powerful as what they are facing."

"Is the FX9 still in the villa?"

"Yes."

"Good, get me the locations of the guards in the villa that are firing at the attackers. Also, let's get that BZ20 activated. Does Jimmy have a silencer on his weapon?"

"Yes."

"Good. Tell Jimmy to take out the guy firing at the terrace door and that you are giving back up with the BZ20 if he needs it. If Jimmy doesn't take him out, use the BZ20 armed with that dart to do it. Otherwise, we save it." The entire time he was talking, Quint was passing out the Heckler and Koch HK416D assault rifles, the AN/PVS night vision goggles, and a MBITR for him and Buster. He handed extra ammo clips to both men. All three checked their weapons. Next the three men strapped on bullet proof vests. That done, Quint and Buster activated the MBITRs. In the background they could hear Freddy telling Jimmy the plan.

"Guiseppe, can you handle the Heckler and Koch?'

"No problem. I use similar gun in army. This better."

"Here's the plan. We're going over the wall in back where the killers and Jimmy went over. Once inside the grounds, we will synchronize so we all hit at once. Buster, you and Guiseppe will take down the ones at the backdoor. When Jimmy has cleaned up the terrace, he'll back me up out front. Whatever you do, don't go inside until I give the signal. The Owens' guards in the villa have no way to know who we are and why we are in this fight. At this point, they could fire on us just as easily as the others."

"Freddy, I have a rough layout of the villa, but I need you to be my eyes in there. Keep that FX9 in the vicinity of the room where Lila is being held. Once we clear the exterior, get the BZ20 in the villa as well. If anyone goes near her door, before we can get in, take them out with that drone. I don't care which side of the fight they belong to. Once inside, I'll give you a signal on the radio."

"You all set here and know what to do?" Both Guiseppe and Buster nodded. "And Freddy, don't come in unless it looks desperate. We need you on those drones."

"Gotcha. And good luck!" Freddy held his fingers up in a victory sign.

The three men donned night vision goggles as they exited. Leaving the van at a running crouch, they quickly gained the back wall. A grappling hook with a rope still hung there. As they prepared to go over, Quint gave them a rough idea of the layout of the villa interior. "Remember the back hall connects by a doorway with the front hall and foyer. Don't enter the villa until I give you the all clear. Once you take out the attackers, warn whoever is shooting from the back door that we aren't part of the assassination team and are here to help. Hopefully, they will believe you, but make damned sure they do before you try to go in."

"Ten four," Buster acknowledged. "Guiseppi, I will go over first, then Quint. You come up last if I signal you it's safe."

"Yes. I understand." Guiseppi swallowed hard. It was true he had served in the army and knew how to handle weapons, but he had never been in an armed, close-combat situation. Squaring his shoulders, he nodded his head. He could do it. Besides, it was something he could brag about to his grandchildren someday...how he had rescued the CIA. Now that was a story.

Ignoring the gunfire both inside and outside the villa, the three men dropped over the wall. Guiseppe glanced at the bodies of the dead guards and the dogs and shook his head. Seeing his focus, Quint remarked in a soft voice, "It's a shame. Those men were just working for a living. I wonder if they realized how deadly guarding Owens was going to be. At any rate, let's focus on what we need to do."

All three men studied the garden and grounds in the rear of the villa looking for cover to maneuver undetected. Quint whispered, "Buster, I'll leave you two to take care of the back entrance. Wait for my signal and then open fire. If it looks like the assassins are getting the upper hand don't wait for me, take them out. Freddy will fly the BZ20 drone over to back you up. I'm going to the terrace area to see what's happening with Jimmy. As soon as that's clear, the two of us will take cover in front. Once we are in position, I'll radio you and we'll open fire at the same time."

"Right." Buster nodded his head to his left, and keeping his voice down, said, "We're going to skirt around through the shrubs along the wall until we have line of sight on the rear door. Good luck."

"You, too, my friend. Let's take'em out." Quint whispered as he moved off in the opposite direction. He was thankful that the moon was not yet up and that it would not be a full moon. The darkness was a blessing. Slipping his night vision goggles down, he moved carefully through the concealing darkness avoiding twigs that might snap and divulge his location. When he neared the terrace, he could see Jimmy crouched behind a large bush. He clicked his radio to let him know he was moving in. Crouching beside Jimmy, he mouthed, "You clear here."

Jimmy gave the all clear signal with his hand and pointed toward the still body of one of the hired killers. Holding up two fingers, he pointed towards the rear of the villa and then towards the front.

Quint nodded in comprehension. Four assailants left. Whispering, he told Jimmy that Buster had the rear entrance covered. Spotting a dark area on Jimmy's shirt, he leaned over and touched him on the arm. His fingers came back sticky. "Hey man, have you been hit?"

Jimmy looked down at his left arm and shrugged, "He winged me before I could nail him. Don't worry, it's not fatal."

"No, but you're bleeding pretty steadily. Hold still while I tie a handkerchief around it."

When Quint tightened the handkerchief over the wound, Jimmy swore, "Damn. I'd rather you'd just left it alone."

"Hey, don't be a wimp. You ready to move in?"

"Let's do it."

Moving off to his right with Jimmy huddled close behind,

Quint began to work his way to the front of the villa. As they crawled through the bushes, Jimmy knocked over some metal that made a loud clang. "Dammit," he swore under his breath as one of the guards turned their way and began to spray the bushes with bullets.

"Make a run for those big pots. I'll cover you."

Quint laid down fire while Jimmy ran. When Jimmy reached the first large urn, he began to fire as Quint ran up to the other.

Crouching behind large topiary urns on each side of a set of steps that led to a short walkway to the front entrance, Quint and Jimmy got into firing position. Activating his radio, he keyed in Buster and Freddy. He ordered Buster to wait for the count of three to clear the rear entry. Freddy would provide them back-up in the rear by firing the BZ20 at the two assailants in back using the explosive device setting. When Quint had acknowledgement from both, he began the count down. He signaled to Jimmy to take the assassin on the left while he zeroed in on the one on the right. Before they could get off a shot, they watched one of the defenders inside the front door of the house fall to the floor. He had obviously been hit by the assailants. At the count of three they opened fire on the two attackers who were instantly taken out in the crossfire. The explosion in the rear of the villa followed by sporadic gunfire occurred simultaneously with their frontal assault. He radioed Buster for a status report.

"It's clear here. We're holding until you tell us what to do next. Best we can tell, the guard at the back entrance was killed just before the BZ20 targeted the shooters with the load of C4. One had died instantly from the explosion. The other was injured but managed to get off a few more rounds before Guiseppe took him out with a crack shot between the eyes."

"Okay. Hold your position until I give further orders."

Quint was desperate to know if anyone was left alive inside, where they were, and what threat they posed to his wife. Calling Freddy, he asked, "Can you get that FX9 moving and the BZ20 rearmed? Check the aerial surveillance feed for any heat signatures. I need to know where any survivors are STAT!"

"The FX picks up a man in the front foyer moving towards the room you think Lila is in. The kitchen help is huddled in the pantry. It looks like all the guards were either killed or badly wounded. I can't tell their exact status from here. They're all down, at any rate. The same for the assassins."

"Okay. Get the FX9 into the room if that guy opens the door.

"That's not a problem, but I have to bring the BZ20 back to rearm it, so it'll be a few minutes before it can do you any good."

Quint immediately radioed Buster and ordered Guiseppe and him to rush the back entrance ready to clear the area if they encountered opposition. He then turned to Jimmy and said, "It looks like there is only one uninjured survivor, and he is headed for the room where we think they are holding Lila. The others are all dead or seriously wounded because they aren't moving. We're going in. I'll go first. Cover me."

"Right."

Dashing to the door, Quint ignored the bodies surrounded by pools of blood as he stepped around them. Looking down the front hall, he spotted a man unlocking and entering the room where he suspected Lila was held. With fear for her pumping adrenalin through his veins, he dashed into the villa with Jimmy on his heels. Clicking over to Buster as he ran, he ordered, "If you guys have finished checking the rear area, come to the front hall for backup."

"No one here but the cook and a helper. They aren't armed and are both shaking with fear. All they want to do is get the hell out."

"Better tell them to stay put until we are finished here. We may need to talk to them at some point. Just reassure them they're safe and we mean them no harm."

"Freddy, did you get the FX9 into the room where Lila is?"

Chapter 15

Lila was still struggling to retrieve the remote for the Murphy bed, when she heard the lock turning in the door followed by it closing. She instantly froze, straining to hear who was there…the assassins or someone else. She heard footsteps as the intruder opened the bathroom door and went in. Immediately the person came back into the room.

It was Owens. "Mrs. Cord, you have to be in here. I will not harm you. I need you to come out so we can leave the villa. My guards are all down; at least three are dead and two badly injured. I'm going to phone for an ambulance for them, but I want to be gone from here before it arrives. I really don't want to be involved with the police when they find all of these dead bodies."

Lila debated with herself. If she answered, she would still be his prisoner. If she didn't, who would rescue her? No, she decided. Let him leave. Eventually she hoped she would be able to retrieve the remote and free herself. If not, when the police arrived, she would call out.

Lyon Owens stood in the center of the room and slowly turned. There was nowhere for the woman to hide and no way out except through a locked door. How could she have gotten free? Would his assistant have freed her before he stationed himself in the front hall? If he had, was the woman hiding somewhere in the villa? Surely, she would not have left the relative safety of the villa to go into grounds that were filled with gunmen. Either way, he could not afford the time it would take to search for her. He needed to be gone and fast. He would prefer to take her with him, but if that were not the case, he still had to protect himself first. He could always find another way to stop Ogden's ability to hire assassins.

Shrugging his shoulders in resignation, Owens was turning to leave the room when the door burst open. Whirling, he found himself face to face with a gun leveled at him by an unknown man. Never taking his eyes from the assault rifle, Owens asked, "What do you want? If you are one of Ogden's men, just go ahead and shoot."

The man growled, "Drop the gun. Now! On the floor and spread eagle."

"Okay, okay," Owens muttered as he obeyed the order. "Who are you? What do you want?"

"I'm Quint Cord with the CIA, as are these men with me that just saved your sorry ass." Quint pointed to the others who had now joined him in the room. "Now, you answer my question: what have you done with my wife? If you have harmed her in anyway, I swear I'll kill you."

His face had drained of color the moment he heard Quint's name. "No matter what you think of me, I would never do that. Your wife must have gotten out somehow during the attack. Perhaps, my assistant freed her. I looked in the bathroom and she isn't there, and as you can see, she's not in here."

"Hold on." Quint keyed his radio to pick up Freddy, "Hey, man. Scroll back through the video on the FX9 and see if Lila left this room."

"I don't need to go back. I've been watching it the whole time. She never left."

"Okay, thanks." Quint turned to Owens, "She's here. She

must be hiding. Is there anywhere large enough to hold her?"

"Look for yourself. I checked the bathroom and the closet, plus the cabinets under the desk. She's not here."

"What's that large wall cabinet?"

"That's a Murphy bed. That folds up flat against the wall. If she were in there, it wouldn't close."

"Can you open it?"

"Yes, of course. There is a remote control for it. It has to be here somewhere."

After a thorough search of the room, no remote could be found by any of them.

"That's it. She has to be in there," Quint exclaimed. Going to the Murphy bed, he pounded against the door and hollered, "Lila, can you hear me?"

Almost sobbing in relief, she replied, "Thank God! Yes, but I dropped the remote and can't get out. Can you open the cabinet doors?"

"Hold on."

Before he could ask if there was another remote, Owens commented, "The only remote is in there with her and that's a steel door. Her air will run out before we can break it down."

"Lila, you're going to have to try to fish that remote out and use it. It's the best way out. Are you okay? Do you have enough air?"

"It's getting stuffy and it's hot. I'm on top of the bed and there's not much room. The remote is where I can touch it with my fingertips, but I can't get a grasp on it. I'll try again to reach it."

"Good girl. Take your time. Do you have anything you can use to help bring it up?"

"Oh, wait. I have a hair barrette."

"Great, use it on one side and your finger on the other and see if you can pull it to you."

An anxious five minutes passed as the men waited in silence for Lila to retrieve the remote. With his ear pressed against the cabinet, Quint could hear her cursing with frustration. Just as he was ready to try another route to free her, the motor that operated the bed began to whine. As the doors opened, Lila struggled to climb back onto the top surface of the bed to keep from falling to the floor. She had just gotten half on when she felt herself being plucked from the bed and into someone's arms.

"You're safe, babe. I've got you now and I'm not letting you go for a long time." Quint smiled down into her face just before leaning forward and kissing her.

"You guys are supposed to be the best. What took you so long?" She could not help teasing a little now that she was safe.

Buster chuckled, "Considering…when it happened…we didn't know the how, who, why, or where, I think we did pretty well."

Quint stood Lila on her feet before turning back to Owens. "You've got a real mess out there, and we don't plan to be around for the mop up. Before you think you're off the hook, let me assure you, you're coming with us."

"That's fine. I wasn't planning to stick around either." Owens stared him in the eye, "I would like to call an ambulance for the two guards that are injured before we go. And someone needs to check on the women in the kitchen. I want them to stay here to take care of the villa for me since I suspect I'm under arrest." It wasn't a question.

"We'll take care of that. I feel sure the ambulance personnel will call police, unless your neighbors have already done it. We need to move guys. Jimmy, cuff him."

The men and Lila walked to the van where Freddy was waiting. He looked up when they entered and said, "I just got off the phone with Director Williams. He was watching the live feed as this went down. He is sending a team here to mop up. I'm to keep him posted until the team arrives and then bring in the drones. I need someone to collect the two injured guys if there is a chance of saving them. The local cops are not going to be involved for political reasons. Switzerland is a neutral country with very particular laws about pseudo-military style operations by outsiders. He says the President does not want the CIA tied to this mess. The corpses are going to disappear in the lake. It's certainly convenient that the villa is on Lake Lugano. In a few days after the fish go at them, their own mothers won't recognize them. We have a doctor we can trust that is going to meet us in Lugano to treat the two injured men."

Quint pointed towards Jimmy, "Him, too. That arm will probably need stitches."

Buster turned to Guiseppi and signaled, "Come with me and we'll see if these guys are fatally injured or if they can be saved."

"Did the Director say how he wants us to handle Owens?" Quint asked.

"He didn't say much to me, but I gather he has some questions for him about Senator Ogden. We are to detain him in Lugano until the team cleans up here. Director Williams said he would call you back in two hours."

"Do we need to wait here?"

"When your driver gets back, you, Lila and Buster can go to the hotel with Owens. Jimmy and I are going to wait for the mop-up team, and then we will take the injured men to the doctor in Lugano. The Director is planning a conference call with President Northrup, Owens, and you guys. It sounds like something big if the POTUS is in on it."

Owens looked as puzzled as the others. He could not imagine why the President would want to question him. He had assumed he was going to be treated like any other criminal that had committed a kidnapping and ordered murders. Furthermore, why did anyone care what he thought about Ogden. He'd be hard pressed to prove that the man was behind the assassins. He had tried that gambit to no avail when his mother was murdered. He no longer had any credibility. Ogden was a respected senator and he himself had just become an arrested criminal. Besides, since taking over the firm Ogden founded, and then selling out, he had no firsthand knowledge of the man.

For the first time since entering the van, Lila spoke up, "Why don't you tell Quint your story, Mr. Owens?"

Quint interrupted, "We did some research, Lila. We know Owens' life story from before he was born, and we have a pretty good handle on the senator. Plus, we have some information concerning Ogden that we need to ask Owens about. We'll get into all of that later."

Buster and Guiseppe returned with the wounded guards. One had suffered a wound to the side of the head that had rendered him unconscious but had not penetrated the skull. He was aware enough to walk out. Hopefully, beyond suffering from a major headache, he would recover. The other guard was far more seriously wounded with a gunshot to the abdomen and Buster and Guiseppe had to carry him out. Freddy wasted no time securing the drones and collecting the equipment Quint and the others had used. While he was doing that, Jimmy was busy applying a pressure bandage to the wounded guard's belly while the other guard was holding a gauze pad to his own head. Seeing they were no longer needed, Quint signaled to the others that it was time to go.

Quint and Lila got into the backseat of Guiseppe's taxi with Quint in the middle to act as a buffer between her and Owens. Buster took the front passenger seat. It was a quiet ride into Lugano with each lost in their own thoughts. When they arrived at the front of the hotel, Buster and Lila got out. Buster then helped Owens from the Taxi. Quint stayed behind for a few moments to thank Guiseppe for his help, pay him for his time, and to warn him to say nothing for the foreseeable future about the events at the villa.

While Guiseppe regretted he could not brag on his role in the dramatics of the day, he reluctantly agreed to secrecy. As an additional sop, Quint promised that Guiseppe would be written up in his report to the CIA and a letter of commendation for his service would be forthcoming from the government of the United States. At that, Guiseppe beamed. He could already envision it hanging in a place of prominence in his home. He decided it might even be fun to say he was sworn to secrecy while hinting that he had been instrumental in a major CIA operation.

With his heart lighter than it had been in a long time, Quint entered the hotel to find the others waiting in the lobby. Taking Lila's arm, they walked to the elevator followed by Buster and Owens.

Looking down at himself, Buster exclaimed. "I've got blood all over me. It's a wonder the hotel management didn't say something."

"Take a shower and get on some clean clothes. Lila and I will take Owens to my room. As soon as you're decent again, join us while we wait for the conference call with Washington."

Chapter 16

President Northrup was angry. It was obvious to Quint by the terse acknowledgement when CIA Director Williams linked him into their conference call. The POTUS wasted no time getting to the gist of the reason for the call. Owens was waiting in the bathroom with Buster guarding the door. At some point, Quint suspected he would be included in the call. It was not until the President began to lay out his concerns, that Quint realized the reason for the interest in what he had assumed was just the kidnapping of his wife.

Quint had told Gerald Williams about the donation Senator Ogden had made to the organization called AFGU and the tenets of the clandestine group. Other than Ogden and whatever affiliation he might have with them, nothing was known about the members. After reading their game plan for creating a one world group of united nations, the President was sufficiently alarmed to demand a full investigation. Both Lila and Quint were ordered to work with the CIA Director to ferret out the members and any ties to those in the U.S., particularly any in the government or military. Quint did not have the temerity to suggest he was on his honeymoon and that they had decided to leave the CIA when they married. When the President gave an order, he was enough of a patriot not to disobey.

The President continued, "This is top secret. I need to know who is involved and just how far along they are in reaching their goals. I particularly want to know what Nicholas Ogden has to do with this group, and if any other government officials are involved. The Director will provide any assistance you need. Director Williams, are we ready to put this Lyon Owens on the line? Hopefully he can provide a starting point."

Quint signaled Buster to bring Owens in the room. Switching the phone to speaker, he leaned back in his chair. Lila was beside him, and sensing he was upset, reached over to hold his hand. He whispered, "I'm sorry, babe. It looks like our honeymoon just got delayed again."

Lila smiled and shook her head, "As long as I'm with you, I don't care. Just stay close. I'm not up for anymore of the skullduggery involved in kidnapping."

"That's a promise," he assured her. He just hoped it was one he could keep. Their whispered conversation was interrupted when Buster said, "Mr. President,

Lyon Owens is here now."

Northrup began, "Mr. Owens, a number of alarming things have come to my attention, and I need to know what you may know that could help us."

"I will do what I can, but in return, I need some kind of amnesty for the crimes of which you are aware."

"Mr. Owens, the kind of leniency you deserve remains to be seen. Right now, the crimes that you have engineered are enough for either the death sentence or life in prison. I hope you still have enough love for your country to want to protect it from enemies that seek to destroy it. Once we have your full cooperation…and if it leads to information that proves vital to the survival of our country, then we will deal. Until then, I make no promises. Do you understand?"

"I do, Mr. President. Believe me I did not set off on the path of crime originally. Had the death of my mother been fully investigated, had the perpetrators been made to pay, and had my own life not been threatened by numerous attacks, I would not be sitting here now looking for mercy."

Northrup ignored the comment to ask, "Did your former boss at Caspio, Senator Ogden, ever speak to you about a group called AGFU?"

"I know nothing about it. It wasn't until Mrs. Cord hacked into his banking accounts and discovered his donation to the group, that I ever heard of it. I don't know why he would donate. He never discussed anything other than corporate business with me. To say we did not part on friendly terms is an understatement. Hell, I totally believe he is responsible for my mother's death, the attempt to burn the house in Menton, and numerous attempts on my life here in Lugano. If your Special Ops team had not arrived when they did, I would be a dead man. I would love to be able to prove that he was behind it all."

"Mr. Owens do you not find it strange that the man would go to such lengths to destroy you?"

"I learned years ago that he resented my ancestors' connections to his. Mine were Russian aristocrats, and his were peasants on one of their estates. From the moment he realized who I was, he made my life miserable. That's why I worked to edge him out of his company. He left Caspio with enough money to move to California and ingratiate himself into the politics there. That is the sum of any knowledge I have of what he has or has not done since I maneuvered him out."

"We need you to think about that folder you took. I understand it contained financial accounts and their numbers and those are what you kidnapped Mrs. Cord to hack. Was there anything else in that folder that might trigger the kind of violence against you that you describe?"

"There were some other papers that did not really interest me. I started to trash them, but for whatever reason I shoved them back in the folder. I put all of them in a safe at my villa in Menton. They are still there. The only thing I was out to do was put a stop to the funds that allowed Ogden to continue threats against my life. I know deep down in my gut he had my mother killed. I know he has tried to kill me. I can't prove it in a court of law, but if you look at the funding of the recent assassins that attacked my villa here, you will see it traces back to Ogden. Mrs. Cord was able to ascertain to whom the recent transactions went …one to AGFU and one to a well-known assassin. I have to believe that assassin is the one that organized the attack on my villa that left most of my guards and my personal assistant dead."

Northrup responded, "The CIA will follow that connection and for the moment, we will keep your villa in Switzerland out of any official inquiries. That is all I can offer you until we know more."

"One more thing, Sir."

The President hesitated before asking, "What?"

"My maids are accustomed to caring for the villa. Other than a bad fright, they are unharmed. The guard with the head wound should be well enough to return there as well. The other guard is in serious condition. I want to see that his expenses are covered, and his salary is still being paid until he also can return to the villa and that the others continue to receive their salaries. I need to add more money to the household account as well. Will you permit me to make those arrangements for my staff?"

His answer was a sharp, "You are going to be incommunicado for the time being. But I will arrange for Mrs. Cord to do that for you by an online transfer of funds. If the money is transferred to your household account, do you have someone designated to handle the account?"

"My cook."

"We'll see it's taken care of."

"Thank you, Sir."

"I want you to cooperate with Mr. Cord. They will take you under custody to your villa in Menton. You will turn over to Mr. Cord the Ogden records you took when you left the Caspio corporation. Will you comply?"

"I will."

"You are dismissed, Mr. Owens."

"Yes, Sir."

The President continued, "Director Williams and Mr. Cord, I need the two of you on the line without Mr. Owens knowledge of what we discuss. Have him removed to a secure location."

Buster stood and motioned to Owens to follow him back to the bathroom. When the door was closed behind them and Quint heard the water running to drown out any sound, he said, "You may continue. My wife is here and will overhear. If that is a problem, she will leave."

The POTUS responded, "That's fine. I suspect we are going to need her expertise as we continue to track the AFGU organization. We need to know who the members are and how far along they are in their aims. It is critical to know if any other congressmen or women or members of our national security agencies, investigative agencies, and judiciary are involved. I want that file he has in the villa in Menton. If it has a link to members in this group, you will need to pursue it as quickly and thoroughly as possible."

"Fine, sir. Now, what do you want us to do?"

Northrup directed, "Director Williams, you can take it from here. I'm needed in a Cabinet meeting."

Gerald replied, "I can handle it, sir."

When the President was off the line, Gerald continued, "We will have a guard posted at the villa in case a new assassin team shows up. When this one doesn't report back to whomever hired them, he could well send another team to finish the job. As for you, Quint, Lila, and Buster…I want you to stick to Owens like white on rice. As you just heard, the President is most anxious to learn the principle players in AFGU and how that ties into Ogden. We need to sift through that file for anything that might provide some insight. Until then, we need to keep Owens safe as he is a direct link that we may need to use to trap the Senator and anyone else in governmental positions…right down to the military and ambassadorial staffs. Keeping Owens safe is going to be your job, Buster.

"Lila you will take care of transferring funds to the villa account, and I need you to continue monitoring the Senator's online activities. We have a wiretap on his phone to track any calls he makes that will trigger an alert within the CIA…those to foreign nationals for example. We may need all of you to go after anyone we find. If additional assets are needed, you will have them.

"Quint, I need you to get that file from his house in Menton. If it is not there, find it. If Owens is stalling for time by saying the file is in that villa and it really is somewhere else…or no longer exists, we need to know ASAP. If you do find it, sift through for anything pertaining to AGFU and get back to me. Also, send me the original of any pertinent papers and make a copy for your use. Are there any questions?"

Quint look at Buster and Lila who both shook their heads in the negative, "No, sir."

"Good, now let's get on it. It's getting late tonight and I know you are tired, but first thing in the morning, drive to Menton and secure that file."

After they got off their phones, Buster retrieved Owens from the bathroom and took him to his own room where the man would be handcuffed to the bed. Once they had left, Quint drew Lila into his arms and kissed her.

"I am so sorry you had to go through this, babe."

"So am I. It surely wrecked a perfectly good honeymoon.'

"Let's just call it a temporary setback." Quint smiled, but Lila could see the worry behind his eyes.

"You know, this is a beautiful place to visit sometime, but the minute we are finished with this mess, I just want to go home to Figure Eight and see Code and Teresa. That's as good a place to honeymoon as anywhere. Besides, I feel safe there. Furthermore, if we don't get home soon that dog of yours just may decide to come after us."

"I've been calling to check on things with Teresa, and she always puts Code on the phone to hear my voice. His barks are getting a little sharper each time I call."

"I will be glad when we are back on the beach watching him chase sand fiddlers."

"So will I." Quint winked at Lila when he continued, "Can we have a practice run on our honeymoon? I've been missing my bride."

Lila's answer was to begin unbuttoning his shirt. They fell asleep a couple of hours later with Quint curled protectively around his wife. Twice her life had been threatened by their association with the CIA. He could not risk it happening again. Somehow, he would keep her safe until the AFGU problem was solved. After that, the government would need to find another hacker.

Chapter 17

Quint was sleeping soundly when the phone blared from the bedside table. Shaking his head to clear it, he reached over for the receiver, "Hello."

Freddy exclaimed, "Sorry to wake you, but this can't wait. When the mop up crew arrived to clean up the bodies and the residue, they found that one of the assassins had crawled off. Looks like they weren't all dead like we thought. They tracked him into the woods where they found his body. He had a phone in his hand and appears to have made a call before he died…I would guess he called whoever hired them to let them know that the kill team screwed up."

"Damn, that means someone could still be out there trying to take Owens out. Put one of the assets from the Milan office on getting into the phone and see if they can find who the man called."

"We already have a man working on it. In the meantime, Buster, Jimmy and I are rotating in four-hour shifts to guard the hall outside our rooms."

"Give me a minute to get dressed, and I'll take the next shift."

"No rush, Buster just took the first shift. If you want the one after, set your clock for a little under four hours from now."

Quint hung up the phone and lay back on his pillow. The news meant that they could not afford to let their guard down for a single moment until they got the file from Owens' safe. They could all be in peril while Owens was in their custody. He and the other men were accustomed to facing danger, but he hated the very idea of exposing Lila to anything further. Yet, with the President's directive, none of them had any choice but to continue digging into AFGU and Senator Ogden's connection to the clandestine organization.

Lila murmured something in her sleep, and Quint rolled over to whisper in her ear that all was okay. For him, there was no more sleep. It was almost a relief when his watch signaled time to get up, dress, and take his station in the hall. Lila did not stir as he rolled from bed, felt for his clothes in the dark and left the room. Buster glanced up when he entered the hall and smiled in welcome.

"Hey, man, I'm so damned tired of sitting in this chair I could scream. Looks like this Owens job is not going to be a piece of cake after all. You packing heat?"

"Yeah." Quint held up his Glock. "This ought to do."

"If nothing else it will make a hell of a mess if someone tries to fuck with us. Not to worry, I have your back. The minute I hear anything I will be here to back you up."

"That's good to know. Now, you need to get some rest. As soon as it's light, we're going to leave here and head for Menton. I think we are all going to feel a whole lot better when we get our hands on that file. If there's nothing in it, that is more reason to keep Owens alive. He is our best access to whatever is going on because of his connection to the Senator."

"I agree. You know, I don't think what he's done is right and it doesn't justify kidnapping Lila and ordering the guys that snatched her to be killed, but I can kind of understand where the guy is coming from. If my life were on the line, I wouldn't have too many limitations on what it took to stay alive, especially when my mother had been murdered in order to get to me."

"Yeah, I get it. But that bastard kidnapped my wife. I'm not feeling too forgiving right now."

"Try not to stew. Just remember we need him to retrieve that file for us. See you in four. Right now, I just want to get a little shut eye." Buster turned back outside his door, "By the way, I let him use his cell phone to call the villa and give the cook instructions about taking care of it while he's away."

"I don't know if that was wise or not. I guess we will have to see if the hired goons pick up on it. At any rate, too late now to worry. Thanks for keeping him in your room, Buster. I needed some 'us' time with Lila. She puts up a brave front, but I can feel just how terrorized she was." Quint paused before adding, "You realize, there is no one I would rather have as back up than you."

"You got it. Okay, then, I'm off to check my eyelids for pinholes. You need me, holler."

"Will do."

Quint settled into the seat that Buster had just vacated. It was still warm from his body heat. Resting his weapon across his legs, he schooled himself to stay alert. Around him were the typical noises of the night. Someone in a nearby room was snoring loudly enough to wake the dead. In the distance, he could hear the traffic in front of the hotel muffled by windows that deadened sound. At three in the morning, the sounds were all typical for the hour.

The next hour found Quint shifting in the chair as he struggled to stay, not only awake, but alert. He was unhappy that Owens had used his cell phone, and he fully intended to take it from him come morning. They did not need any more killers coming after the man while he was in their custody. At four, Freddy showed up looking his usual cheerful self.

"Damn, if that were my bride in there," he pointed to Quint's room, "I for sure wouldn't be sitting out here. I thought Jimmy was to stand guard after Buster."

"I took the rotation for him. After getting wounded, I figured he needed the rest."

"I suspect so. He's still sleeping like the dead judging from the snores I hear coming from his room."

"Are you good to roll as soon as the others are up and ready to go?"

"Yeah, Jimmy and I are going to take the van and head for Milan. We need to check into the agency. If you need us, all you need to do is call and we will join you in Menton."

"Hopefully, that will not be necessary. However, I am a little concerned that Buster let Owens make a call to his villa here. If someone is seriously tracking him, that could be a give-away to his location."

"Oh, hell. Buster should have known better than that."

"Tell me about it. Thing is, I think he likes the guy and kind of understands where he is coming from."

"That doesn't sit well with me. I tell you what, I just changed our plans. Jimmy and I are going to follow you into Menton and stay with you until you get that folder. I will let the Director know that we are taking a detour rather than going straight to our office in Milan. If another assassination group comes after Owens, you are going to need more than you and Buster if it is anything like the last bunch."

"I appreciate that. The sooner we get that file, the sooner I can get Buster and Owens on a plane to D.C. Then it becomes Gerald's problem to keep him safe while they milk him for information."

Freddy remarked, "I think it is strange that until Lila hacked into the senator's account and caught the money transfer to AFGU, no one had ever heard of it. I don't know if it is some insignificant bunch of pseudo-elitist intellectuals that think they know what's best for the world, or if it is a powerful bunch of thugs that are out to take over the USA and other countries. Hell, if our country falls, the other free nations of the world will come down like a house of cards."

"That's why we must keep Owens alive until we get that folder and can figure out what's going on. If it weren't for that, I would say to hell with protecting him after what he put Lila through."

"Can't say that I blame you, Quint. At any rate, get yourself a few minutes of shut eye. I arranged for the front desk to give our rooms an eight o'clock wake up call."

"Goodnight, Freddy. And, thanks again for your help. It was invaluable."

"Just doing my job. But, you're welcome. It just feels good to know that we rescued Lila with only Jimmy getting a minor wound in the process."

"For sure," Quint agreed as he crossed the hall to his room.

Quint slipped into bed beside Lila. She stirred in her sleep but did not awaken. He was sleepy but knew he would not be able to doze off. To pass the time, he began to go through the series of events that led to this point, beginning with the newspaper article featuring Lila as a renowned hacker. He was proud of her skills, admired her acumen and intellectual ability, adored her sass, and was enthralled by her physical beauty; but he continued to regret that he had ever bragged to Gerald Williams about her ability to hack into the underbelly of the World Wide Web. Not only did that make her invaluable to the CIA, but it also put a target on her back for people like Owens to come after her for nefarious purposes.

His thoughts wandered to Senator Ogden's donation to AFGU and what connection that had to Owens. It was possible that there was none and the attempt against Owens' life was some personal vendetta on the part of Ogden. If so, likely there would be nothing in the file in Menton, and the attempts on the man's life were just that and nothing more. That would give them nothing to go on to identify Ogden's compatriots except what Lila might get lucky enough to hack.

From time to time, Freddy walked the hall from one end to the other to stay awake. The hotel was quiet in the rooms along the hallway. An occasional snore or cough was all that interrupted the still of the night. Just before dawn, distant sounds of the kitchen coming to life preceded the smell of coffee and other breakfast items. His stomach growled in appreciation. He would make sure they all had time for breakfast before the drive to Menton.

At seven, Buster emerged from his room dressed and ready to go. "Looks like you had a quiet night."

"So far, so good. Is Owens dressed and ready?"

"Yeah, he's all set. I left him handcuffed to the radiator so he's not going anywhere until we're all ready to go down to breakfast. I don't think Owens wants to leave our protection any way, despite what punishment the law may have in store. That man is scared senseless of these hired thugs that continue trying to kill him."

"Good. I hope he stays that way. I'm going to grab my stuff and be ready to roll."

"See you in a few."

After a hurried breakfast in the hotel dining room, Buster got in the driver's seat of the rental car with Lila in the front passenger seat. Quint and Owens seated themselves in the rear seats. Freddy and Jimmy pulled out behind them in the Agency van. Leaving Lugano, traffic was light, and they made good time to the autostrada to Milan. By the time they reached the rest stop, an hour or so past Genoa, it was time to stop for a bite to eat and restrooms. None of them noticed the grey Mercedes that pulled up not long after them. Three men in dark suits also entered the rest area restaurant.

In forty minutes, they were back in their vehicles and ready for the drive to Menton along the Ligurian Coast. Owens sat in deep thought, ignoring the others. Blindfolded during her trip to Lugano, Lila was now enjoying the view and remarking to Quint about the passing landscape. Quint had little to say other than to respond to her comments and to promise to return someday when they could enjoy the locale. A feeling in his gut that something wasn't right was making him nervous. He had learned to always trust his instincts. That inner sense had saved his life on numerous occasions.

It wasn't until Buster said, "I can't be sure, but I think I saw that same grey sedan that is behind us pull out when we left the rest area. They got in between the van and us several kilometers back and are staying glued to our tail. We are going to be coming to tunnels and some curving sections of the road shortly and that makes me nervous to have someone hugging our bumper."

Quint looked back at the car behind them. "I'll call Freddy and tell him we're going to speed up and for them to try to pass the grey car. If the car speeds up, too, then we can slow down to see if it will pass us. You cool with that, Buster?"

"Got it." While Quint talked to Freddy, Buster was steadily

increasing their speed. The grey car was keeping pace leaving no room for the van to pull in. Buster then began to lower their speed. The Mercedes slowed and made no attempt to pass.

The cat and mouse game continued with the Mercedes staying firmly behind them. Traffic was beginning to thin out after they went through the long tunnel near Ventimiglia. Here the road was elevated in numerous places with sheer drop offs. Buster's grip on the steering wheel tightened. By this time everyone in the car was in the grip of nervous tension.

Just as they entered a sharp curve, the Mercedes pulled alongside. Quint saw the man in the back seat lower his window and stick out an automatic pistol. He immediately pulled Lila down into the seat while warning Buster. Immediately Buster slammed on brakes, and the car shot pass them. The man in back was joined by another in the front who began firing an automatic at their car. Buster began evasive swerving maneuvers, but two bullets penetrated the front windshield and buried themselves in the upholstery mere centimeters from Owens.

Quint lowered his window and fired several shots from his Glock but did not hit the car. By this time, Freddy and Jimmy had pulled alongside in the van. Despite his injury, Jimmy fired a volley of high-powered rounds at the Mercedes. The shots shattered the back windshield and appeared to have wounded the man in back. He ceased firing as blood spattered the window and slumped from view. At that point, the sedan raced away from them. Everyone in their group breathed a sigh of relief. It was apparent to them all that whoever was after Owens had not given up. The remainder of the drive into Menton was uneventful, but even so, the people in both vehicles were wary of every vehicle that came up behind them or passed.

Chapter 18

Nicholas Ogden paced his elegantly furnished office, walked from behind the highly polished burled walnut desk to the damask draped window that overlooked the rear grounds of his mansion. He stared out without seeing. Normally, he would have delighted in the beautiful private lake with a fountain that jetted water high into the air, but now it did not even register on his conscious mind. He gnawed at the thumbnail of his right hand until the nail was torn down into the quick. He was unaware of the pain as he continued biting until the metallic taste of blood made him stop. Owens possessed the uncanniest luck of anyone he had ever known. Despite sending some of the best assets in the world for clandestine operations, the man had managed to elude them all.

Shaking his head with disgust, he stared balefully at the phone on his desk. He was furious. He could not imagine how the government knew of AFGU, or even if they did. He did not know how his cohort in AFGU, Reginald Henderson...former Representative from California, former Ambassador to the U.N., and now Vice President in President Northrup's second term, had gotten wind of his attempt to murder Owens. Henderson could have someone in Switzerland on his payroll that learned of it and told him. In his role as Vice President., he might have learned of the attempt against Owens. Perhaps, he had learned it from the CIA or POTUS himself. The latter was unlikely as he had angered President Northrup by speaking out against several of Northrup's decisions and a definite chill existed between them resulting in Henderson's exclusion from many meetings. That left someone on the cabinet or in the President's office staff that was in Henderson's paid employ to provide any information that might threaten AFGU if the information had come from that quarter. Regardless of how he knew, that call made it plain that Ogden was the one with a target on his back if his fellow members of AFGU were compromised. They would not hesitate to throw him under the bus while they ran for cover. Besides, the others were foreign nationals whose governments would disavow any knowledge of their activities.

If the last three he hired to kill Owens failed, he did not know what to do next. No sooner had that entered his mind than his phone rang again. He debated with himself whether to answer it. He did not need any more ass chewing from the other principals of AFGU. On the tenth ring, he could take it no more. Snatching up the phone he snarled, "What?"

"He got away again. One of my men is hurt and of no more use. But the one I have left is good. Between the two of us, I promise you we will get him."

The news landed hard leaving Ogden with a pain in his gut. "Schmidt, I have paid good money, but you are having a hell of a time delivering. Don't screw up again. I can't afford it. And, you can't either."

"What in the hell is that supposed to mean? I hope you don't think you can threaten me." Schmidt's laugh was nasty.

Ogden took a deep breath and counted to five. He had to be more conciliatory while he still had need of the man. "No, no. I'm just upset that this is taking so long."

"You think I'm not? I have five dead employees and one that's badly wounded. I think we need to talk about that money again. What you sent doesn't begin to cover my costs. Before I stick my neck any further out, you wire me another fifty K and the promised one hundred K when the job is done."

"That wasn't the deal and you know it. I told you that the rest of the money would be paid when you finished the job."

Schmidt growled, "Losing my men wasn't part of the deal either. So, pay the additional fifty up front, or find another sucker to do your dirty work."

"Hey, your guys knew the risk involved. It's not my fault you screwed up.

"If you don't like the way I handle things, you come do it. Either I get the money now, or I quit."

Ogden was slow to respond, but at last he acknowledged he had no other choice. "I'll send the additional fifty up-front money. No more disappointments. You make sure this time, you hear? And remember, not only do I want him finished off, I also want that file."

"Yeah, yeah."

Ogden was still holding the phone when the line went dead. Looking at it, he realized his hand was shaking. That call was the last problem he needed in a day already fraught with problems. He needed a drink to settle his nerves. Walking to the built-in mirrored bar and taking one of the gleaming Lalique crystal glasses from the glass shelf, he poured a hefty amount of vodka. There was plenty of time to finish his drink before sending more money. At least he had the foresight to change his account numbers from the ones that Owens stole. No more tracing his transactions. At that, Ogden smiled. He walked over to the chesterfield sofa, sat in the corner, and stretched his legs out on the butter soft leather. The first sip of the vodka warmed his belly and sent a pleasant feeling of relaxation into his tight muscles. By the time he had finished the liquor, he was feeling far more sanguine.

Damn, he thought, I wish my grandparents could see me now. Their home brewed vodka made from a crop of gnarly potatoes was a poor second to the top-shelf one he drank. He could still picture the dirt-floored hovel where his father had been born, and then he himself. Looking around the professionally decorated room, he grinned. He had worked hard, made all the right moves, built a name for himself, a vibrant company, and then a political career. The only fly in the ointment was the one man who had ever bested him at anything. Lyon Owens. He almost spat the name. That was the thanks he got for educating the bastard. If he had known the man's lineage, he would never have helped him.

Despite growing up in the U.S., Owens was at heart the aristocratic Russian that represented everything Ogden despised. That class, and all others of similar ilk, needed to be history. The ruling class with their arrogant sense of ingrained superiority squashed all others. There was no room for them in the new world order that AFGU would build. Ogden did not stop to consider that with his Senatorial seat and immense wealth he had achieved the elite rank that placed him in the ruling class. In his mind, despite all outward manifestations of having ascended beyond his roots, he was still of the despised and downtrodden Russian peasant class...the very peasants abused by landlords like Owens' grandparents and great-grandparents for generations past. The Russian revolution had ended the reign of the Tsars, but too many of the Russian nobility had escaped like Owens' parents. As far as he was concerned, their descendants should all die to answer for the crimes of their ancestors. That was just one more justification for ordering the man murdered.

With Schmidt pursuing Owens, it was just a matter of time before that would be one of his problems eliminated. Walking back to his desk, Ogden sat the empty glass beside the keyboard and began the transfer of funds. With that done, he refilled the glass and again stood gazing out the window. In the growing dusk, the lights under the fountain came on adding to the splendor of the view. Taking a large sip of the silky vodka, he contemplated it with satisfaction. His next problem was far more delicate and potentially even more vital to his survival. He needed to know who was the mole that had learned of his attempts against Owens. If he could buy the mole's services, he would have some control over Henderson by cutting him out of the information loop. No matter what happened with Owens and the file, that would give him insurance. However, he could not rely on learning the identity of Henderson's spy alone.

The file...now that would take some mulling over. He needed to think carefully about the members and those that could be leaned on to support him. Henderson would sell him out in a minute to save his own hide. But there were others less vulnerable and so committed they would deny everything, and their governments would back them up.

He began to mentally tick off the members of AFGU. The first, Reginald Henderson, was wealthy and very well connected to his party members because of his generous campaign donations. He could well afford a mole in the CIA. He would bear thinking about, especially considering the threatening phone call. He would get no help from him. Henderson was as vulnerable as Ogden if he were to be exposed as a member of a cabal to overthrow Western Governments. That was especially true if his role, once they began to implement AFGU, were revealed. If they came for him, Vice President Henderson would turn government witness and never look back. Hell, he would probably paint himself as a savior who had joined the cabal just to monitor what they were up to and to thwart any potential plan.

The second, Ukrainian Cabinet Minister, Vadym Peliura, was a holdover from the era of Russian control. He was corrupt and for sale to the highest bidder in Ogden's opinion, and thus should never have been allowed to become a member of the AFGU principals despite his extensive diplomatic record. The fact that he could be bought made him potentially useful as an ally if Henderson turned on him.

Third, The Minister of Labor for France, Georges Blum, represented an increasingly dissatisfied laboring class. He was a solid man, highly idealistic and committed. He was noted for his political skills. He would never jeopardize AFGU. For him, the proposed new world order was the ultimate hope for the French laboring class.

Fourth, Germany's Peter Lambrecht, Minister for Foreign Affairs, now there was an enigma. The man was highly intelligent, well educated, and terse in his comments before the others in AFGU. Ogden wondered if he was solidly committed or merely hedging bets. For that reason, he crossed him off the list of someone that might prove useful, but he would still call him to explain the plan.

The fifth, Italy's Minister of Defense, Marco Bonafede, had real potential. With a propensity for sex with underage girls, he was the most vulnerable of them all. Unfortunately, his military expertise also made him valuable as each member had been chosen for acumen in a particular area.

That left the sixth and final member other than Ogden himself: Sir William MacDonald, England's Secretary of State for Education. With a background in accounting, the Englishman was the appointed treasurer for AFGU. He was another ideolog using his post to push a socialist agenda in his country's schools. He was possibly the most zealous of them all and would head off any serious investigation of AFGU in England. MacDonald might be someone he could use were Henderson to go after him.

Tossing back his third vodka, Ogden reached a decision. A preemptive strike was better than a defense. He would personally call each of the other members and warn them that a file had been stolen from his office that contained their names. That removed the immediate threat that Henderson would get to them first, and it would allow them to build cover. With carefully orchestrated meetings and communications, there was little in the way of concrete evidence that could be used against them if they continued to be discrete. He would not tell them that the file contained the complete implementation plan. There was no way to get around that damning document. As he saw it, there were two ways to play it. First, should one of the others squeal, he could deny any knowledge of the contents of the folder or the other members, or considering the time since its removal, he could try pleading forgetfulness of what it contained should the government question him. The second option was to explain it all away as an evening of heavy drinking where they dreamed it up on a lark but never did anything about it...indeed had forgotten all about it.

That left the damned donation. What poor timing to have wired funds to AFGU. If it had been a drunken joke, how was he to explain sending that much money? If he explained it was a slush-fund they set up that night while they were drunk to help one another when they needed extra cash for investments, could he get the others to agree to that? As he saw it, there was no reason why they should object to the second option as that neatly covered them all. If they stuck to the agreed story, nothing could be proven.

His first call would be to MacDonald to set up the defense for the money transfer that someone had caught him making. After he explained the problem, he felt sure the man would agree to go along with the ruse. They should have considered the traceability of funds long ago. In the current age of technology, little was truly private anymore. Once MacDonald was on board, he would call the others. Lastly, he would call Henderson and tell him how they were going to play it out. He doubted the man would refuse go along. But if he was dumb enough to blab to the government, Ogden would make sure the others hung the Vice President out to dry by making him look like an idiot. Having already ticked off POTUS, Henderson would get no help from that quarter.

From the wall safe in his office, he removed the notepad where he kept phone numbers for AFGU members. Returning to his desk, he began the process of covering his tracks. He did not know it, but Henderson was already beginning to make his move.

Chapter 19

They were sitting around the dining table in Owens' palatial villa in Menton. Having just finished a gourmet meal prepared by the wife of his caretaker, Quint and the others were all relaxed for the first time in days. Owens had called ahead to have the couple, Yvette and Vincent Crenn, prepare the villa for his arrival with guests. By the time they reached the villa, the master suite, and four guest rooms were ready for them and the aromas from the kitchen lured them in. They were all hungry, having eaten little on the road.

Lila's eyes wandered around the dining room landing on two large portraits on the wall behind Owens' chair. When Owens saw the direction of her eyes, he commented, "Those are my parents. The portraits were painted shortly after they fled Russia by the Italian artist, Giovanni Boldini, and installed by him in this very room. It is the only likeness of my parents that I have. The photographs were all destroyed by the fire that was set in the villa when my mother was murdered."

"They were a very attractive couple and obviously very much in love." Lila studied the portrait. "You look like your father."

Lyon Owens took a sip of his wine and nodded, "And, I am told, I resemble my grandfather as well."

"Do you have portraits of your grandparents?" Quint asked.

"No. Unfortunately, my parents were forced to leave them behind when they fled. As it was, they were fortunate to escape with their lives."

Quint was curious, "You say you resemble your grandfather.

I gather Ogden's family were peasants on your family's estate. Didn't the Senator spot the resemblance when he met you?"

"No. It was not until the truth of my parentage came out that he remarked on the similarity of features. His comments were less than complimentary, I assure you."

"So, he has more reason than just the file to come after you. He despises you for your family heritage."

"Absolutely. Of course, I did not endear him to me when I leveraged him out of the company he founded."

Quint was about to respond when the breaking of glass in the window behind him was instantly followed by a red blossoming on Owens' shirt front. The others dived under the table for cover while Buster pulled Owens down. Ripping his shirt open, Buster could see that the wound was in the upper right shoulder just above the lung. While the man was bleeding heavily, it was high enough that it appeared no internal organs were damaged. Quint reached up and felt around the tabletop, ignoring the breaking crystal wine glasses that were being pelted by a volley of bullets. Finding what he was looking for, he handed two napkins to Buster to stanch the bleeding.

"Hang in there, man. You'll be fine as soon as we can get you to a doctor," Quint assured him.

Buster motioned to Lila, "Slide over here and keep pressure on the wound. We don't need to sit here like ducks in a damned shooting gallery. You guys have your weapons on you?"

Both Jimmy and Freddy patted their coats. Their weapons were in their shoulder holsters. Quint pulled his Glock from his waist band.

Buster turned to Owens, "Does your caretaker have a weapon?"

"Yes. I made him get one and learn how to use it after my mother was murdered. I'm sure he went for it when he heard the shots."

Quint ordered, "Lila, I need you to stay with Owens until we can assess the situation and stop whoever is shooting. Owens, is there a safe room in your house?"

Lyon nodded, wincing in pain as he pointed upstairs, "On the second floor in my bedroom. If Lila can help me slide along the floor, I can get us to the hidden stair that leads to my suite."

"Good. Just stay down as you move."

Lila looked at Quint with panic in her eyes, "I don't want to leave you. You promised to stay with me no matter what."

"Right now, sweetheart, the important thing is to get you somewhere safe, so we can stop whoever is out there without worrying about your safety. Will you do that for me?"

Lila nodded. "Okay, but dammit, don't go getting yourself killed."

"I promise. We have a honeymoon to finish sometime." Quint pulled her into his arms and hugged her to him. He only hoped he could keep his promise. Those were some serious bad asses out there.

Lila returned Quint's hug. When he released her, she crawled over to Lyon, "Mr. O, keep pressure on the bandage and lie back. I'll try to slide you to the stairway. Just give me directions when we get out of the dining room."

"Alright."

The others watched as Lila put her arms under and around his armpits, and digging in her heels to pull, ordered him to push with his feet. Despite the agony created by lifting the injured shoulder, he followed her instructions. Once the men saw that the two of them were underway, they crept from under the table and fanned out to the windows. A steady barrage of shots came from the garden behind the villa. From the rear of the house, they heard pistol shots from a small caliber weapon followed by a burst of heavy weapon shots. In seconds, the pistol shots stopped.

Quint looked at Buster, "I suspect we need to cover the rear as it sounds as though the caretaker was taken out."

"Yeah. I'll see to it."

"Freddy, can you stay here and cover the French windows?"

"I will; but kill the damned lights! It's lit up like Christmas in here with all the chandeliers."

"I'll cover the front. Jimmy, I know your wound is bothering you, but we need your help. Could you move to the hall and reinforce wherever you see the need?"

Crawling along the floor, Quint reached the light switch which he quickly reached up and turned off. Buster and Jimmy were right behind him. In the hall, Buster killed those lights as the three men made their way along the floor to their assigned areas.

Buster was almost to the rear of the hall when the door burst open. Rolling to one side he quickly squeezed off a round of shots. He watched as the backlit figure slowly sank to the floor. Crawling to the man, he felt for a pulse…although judging by the headshot his chances were slim. With grim satisfaction, Buster noted that at least one man had just ended his career as a murderer. After grabbing the Swiss SG550 assault rifle, Buster checked the man's pockets for additional clips. He shoved the two he found inside his shirt and continued down the hall, ignoring the growing puddle of blood around the body as he crawled past.

When he reached the rear entry, Buster pulled the body of the caretaker out of the way and slammed the door shut, bolting it securely. He did not take time to admire the French habit of multiple strong locks with bars that reinforced the door. Satisfied that the door was secure, he moved over to Vincent Crenn. The man had received a wound to the abdomen and was moaning in agony. With good medical care he might make it if they could get help soon.

Vincent opened his eyes and looked at Buster, "Please, ma moglie…"

"Your wife?"

"Oui."

Buster called out, "Madame Crenn, venez ici…mais sur la parqueterie." That was the best French he could come up with. He just hoped she could understand him.

Within minutes, a very frightened Yvette peeped around the door and on spying her husband, began to scream.

"Doucement. Quiet please, et assistez moi avec Vincent. Comprenez vous?"

"Yes, yes. I help him now. What I do."

Buster was relieved to switch to English, "Take your apron off and use it to put pressure on his wound. We will get him to a hospital as soon as it's safe. Try not to worry."

Jimmy crawled down the hall to Buster's side. "I think there were just two of them. Once the firing stopped back here, whoever was firing into the dining room stopped. Quint says to lay low for a minute more and he will call for an ambulance for Owens and Mr. Crenn. He and Freddy are checking the grounds now. Hopefully, they will be back in a minute with the all clear."

Buster nodded, "We will have to call the police this time."

Jimmy assured, "Quint's going to do it as soon as we can set things up here. Freddy and I cannot be outed as CIA assets as we are operating undercover. He will try to pass it off as a burglary attempt since until tonight it was just the Crenns here."

"That works. There's no need for the police to think we are anything but tourists and houseguests of Owens."

Jimmy and Buster turned as Quint came towards them followed by Freddy. They flipped on the light switches as they walked.

"Buster, could you fetch Lila and Owens?" Quint asked.

"If I knew where they are, I would?"

"Go upstairs and find his master suite; then holler for them to come out. Tell them that we are all clear. You may have to help get Owens down here if he is weak from loss of blood. I want him here as the owner, so they don't think we just busted in. Tell Owens to say he was just visiting the villa, since he has not been here in a while, and that we are his guests. If he can manage it, we need him to give us that file now before he goes to the hospital. I will stall the police while you are at it. Just make it fast!"

Buster tore down the hall on a dead run and sprinted up the steps. They needed to get things rolling so the injured men could get help. Running down the upstairs hall, he mentally checked off the rooms that he, Quint and Lila, and Jimmy and Freddy occupied. Ignoring them, he entered the grand double doors at the end of the hall and found himself in a plush sitting room. Through the open door on the right, he spotted a canopied bed that looked like something from a king's palace. He figured he had found the right room. Walking to the middle of the bedroom, he hollered at the top of his voice and then started walking around the room hollering and banging on walls. Suddenly, the large armoire began swinging silently out from the wall nearly knocking him down. Quickly he jumped out of the way and waited for it to fully open.

Lila looked out and exhaled a relieved breath. "Thank goodness it's you. Is it okay to come out now?"

"Yeah, go on down to Quint. I'll see to Owens." Buster walked over to where Owens was sagged into a chair. "Is the file in the villa here? We need it fast, because Quint is going to call the police and you're going to need to go to a hospital."

"No."

"No, what?" Buster glared at him.

"No hospital. Get a doctor here for me. I'm a lot safer with you guys, than in the hospital. I'll give you the file after you get me a doctor."

"You've got to go down and talk to the police. How do you think you can hide the fact you've been shot?"

"There are some large bandages in the bathroom mirrored cabinet to the left of the sink. Get them. Then help me out of these clothes and into my smoking jacket. I think I can walk down. You just need to hang onto me and get me settled in the library downstairs. Maybe pour me a shot of liquor while you're at it."

"Hell, I'll pour us both one." Buster chuckled, "You really think you can fool the police?"

"I'm going to try and if you want that file, you have to help me pull it off. Now hurry. My jacket is hanging behind the door in the bathroom.

They heard the doorbell tolling as Buster settled Owens in an ottoman by the fireplace. Leaving him there and with drink in hand, he joined Quint at the front door and explained what Owens planned.

Quint frowned in disgust. "I wish to hell that stubborn fool didn't want to play it this way. Do you think he can pull it off?"

"Looks like our only choice is to help him try if we want that file."

"Right," Quint grimaced when he replied. "By the way, we are passing you off as Owens' bodyguard. Warn him to play along."

The moment Buster reached the library, Quint opened the front door to a group of serious looking policemen all holding weapons at the ready. Constantly glancing over their shoulders and looking around, he could tell the men were nervous. No doubt it was rare to have a disturbance of this kind in the upscale neighborhood.

"Come in, please. We were having dinner when shots were fired into the dining room. I think they were using silencers as only the sound of breaking glass followed by bullets alerted us to what was happening. We suspect that they thought only the caretakers were in residence and it was an easy mark. Judging by the shots, it appears there were just two of them. One is in the rear of the house. He's dead. The other seems to have gotten away. I checked the grounds and could find no one. We are going to need an ambulance as the caretaker has been seriously wounded."

"Are you the owner?"

"No. Lyon Owens is the owner. He's in the library having a drink to settle his nerves. He is understandably upset about Mr. Crenn, the caretaker, as the man has worked for him for many years. The man's wife is with him in the back hall where you will find the body of the burglar that was shot. Except for Mr. Owens' bodyguard, Buster Walton, who is in the library with him, the rest of us are Mr. Owens' guests. Mr. Walton is the man that shot one of the burglars. I'm Quint Cord. My wife Lila and I stopped in on our honeymoon trip. The other two gentlemen are also friends of Mr. Owens and are staying here for a few days."

The officer Quint took for the one in charge spoke up, "Mr. Cord, I am Captain Jacques Brille. I need all of you to meet in the library except for the Crenns. I know Madame Crenn. She is friends with my wife. No doubt, she wishes to stay with her husband."

Dismissing Quint, he turned to his fellow officers and gave orders. "Paul call for an ambulance, and then, get your first aid kit and see what you can do for Mr. Crenn until the ambulance arrives. The rest of you check the grounds and the house for evidence and to make sure no one is still out there."

Chapter 20

Reginald Henderson had never believed in hanging back and waiting. Trusting his gut, he charged ahead when he saw a path to his objectives. The strategy had never failed him as he climbed from a poor boy in the projects to a multi-billionaire. It was that money that had earned him an Ambassadorship and then the Vice Presidency. He always knew which wheels to grease to keep things moving in the right direction. With strategic donations to candidates on both sides of the political divide, he had lots of markers out whenever he needed favors. As Ambassador to the U.N., he had enjoyed a worldwide stage and a valid rationale for his interactions with others in AFGU…even Ogden, as a wealthy and powerful Senator, was a reasonable associate. Just because he could explain his acquaintance with the others, if challenged, did not mean he wanted to go there.

The others might think it was premature to begin implementing the agreed strategy, but with the exposure of Ogden, his instincts told him to act before the CIA could learn more. The second factor weighing heavily on his decision to advance AGFU's agenda was the growing hostility between the President and himself.

His was a bold plan and would take careful planning. The President's upcoming trip to Brussels for a NATO meeting could well be the opportunity he needed to initiate the first step. As the most fervent member of AFGU, Georges Blum would not hesitate to assist him in putting the necessary logistics in place. Each of them had been warned that if the opportunity to initiate the first step occurred in their home country, they were expected to assist in facilitating logistics. He would not be in Belgium during the conference as the President and Vice President could not be out of the country at the same time.

Blum was not only willing to cooperate with his plan; he relished the chance to begin the realization of his dream of a world where all men were truly equalized economically. As an ardent atheist, the outlawing of religions would be an additional bonus. He assured Henderson he knew whom to call to arrange things in Brussels.

Henderson laughed when Blum told him about the call from Ogden. "Don't worry about it, Georges. Senator Ogden's plan is okay as a backup; however, we aren't going to need it. Once we get this done, I will see to it none of you are exposed before we are ready to move to the second stage."

With that part of the operation set in motion, Henderson proceeded to call each of the other members. Judging by their reaction, they found his proposal preferable to waiting to see if they would have to use Ogden's plan. Most of them thought Ogden's idea was wide open for hostile speculation in the media. That would stamp paid to AFGU were it to be revealed before they gained power. Vadynm Peliura's aid was critical. They would rely on him to procure the needed talent.

He dialed the number from his private line and waited until they were connected. "Minister Peliura," he began, "I had not anticipated the need to put our plan in place quite so soon, but recent events give us an unprecedented opportunity to do so."

"Has this anything to do with, Senator Ogden's call to me?"

"In a way it does, which is why it is prudent for us to move our schedule up a bit. What I need to know is whether or not you can get your men to Brussels during the upcoming NATO conference?"

"I assume we are implementing step one?"

"That's right. Can you do it?"

"With this much lead time it should not be a problem."

"Good. Stay in touch. If there are any snags, I need to know immediately."

"Trust me. There will be none."

He hung up with Peliura satisfied that things would progress as planned. That left Senator Ogden. He would call him now and inform him to stand down.

* * * * *

Quint turned to Lyon Owens the moment the doctor, that Director Williams had sent to the villa, left. He was tired of waiting for the promised file. After calling the Director, they had waited for two hours for the doctor to arrive. Despite the intense pain from his wound, Lyon had refused to divulge the location of the file saying that he would not turn it over until he had seen a doctor and had the CIA's promise for protection. Gerald Williams had readily agreed to CIA protection for the foreseeable future but could do nothing to rush the doctor from a scheduled surgery at the local hospital. In the meantime, Buster and Freddy had been out picking up the items that the doctor had said he would need to extract the bullet from Owens' shoulder. The moment the surgery to remove the bullet and sutures were in, the doctor had left, and Owens rested comfortably thanks to a dose of oxycodone. Before he could drift off to sleep, it was time to give over the file.

"We've done everything you have asked. Turn over that file

now, or so help me God, we will walk out of here and leave you to the hired thugs to finish off your sorry ass. I'm in no mood for any further stalling." Quint was still furious with the man for abducting Lila. No matter his reasons for having done so, Owens was on his shit list. Quint didn't expect that to change.

Owens started to rise from his chair, saying, "I'll get it: but hang on to me. That shot made me a little light-headed."

Supporting him by the uninjured left arm, Quint asked, "Where to?"

"The safe room. It's in the wall safe there."

"Buster, I need you to station Freddy and Jimmy in strategic locations around the villa and the three of you keep a sharp watch for any trouble. Hopefully the gunman has cleared off for the moment, but we don't know that for sure. I suspect he won't give up judging by past attempts." Quint thought a moment, "Why don't you call Gerald back and ask if he can arrange a death certificate for Owens and an obituary notice in major French and U.S. papers saying Lyon Owens was killed by an assassin's bullet at his villa in Menton. That should give those that are after Owens some pause."

Owens burst in, "Wait a minute. What about my estate? I don't want my lawyers activating the terms of my will. I'm damned sure not dead, and I don't want to be wiped out financially by some fake obituary."

"Give us the name of the law firm. Gerald can explain what's going on to them and stop any action from that quarter."

"It's Porter and Reeves in Paris. Mr. Reeves wrote my will."

"Okay, Buster, get on it. Owens and I are going for that file."

An hour later, making sure that Owens was sleeping, Quint asked the others to join him in the library. As they settled themselves around the room, Quint walked over and drew the drapes. After shutting the door to the hall, he turned to Lila, Buster and Freddy. Jimmy had agreed to cover the grounds while they met. "I waited so we could go through the file together and determine what to do here before I forward the original to Gerald for further action. Thanks to the copier in his office here, I was able to make a copy for us to keep. I am giving the original to Freddy to put in a CIA pouch for direct delivery. There are several documents in here that all pertain to AFGU. I will go through them. We already know the objectives of the group; what we haven't known is who is involved."

Quint paused to shuffle through the papers, ignoring the ones outlining the basic tenets of AFGU. Finding the one he was seeking, he pulled it out and quickly scanned the page. "Hang onto your seats. You are not going to believe this. It's a shame Owens did not read this and give it to the government. He could have saved himself a lot of trouble."

Lila interrupted, "The suspense is killing me, so get on with it. We all want to know who is involved."

"I have an impatient bride, it seems." Quint smiled before beginning to read. "The current Vice President Joseph Henderson will become the first President of AFGU with the assumption of power in the U.S. quickly followed by the takeover of several other western allies. It looks like Senator Ogden is slated to assume the role of head of the Senate in order to push through legislation to achieve AFGU's aims.

"Georges Blum, Minister of Labor in France will seize the office of President to begin forging an alliance with the U.S. under Henderson. In Germany, Peter Lambrecht, Minister of Foreign Affairs, will take over the government there. The current

Minister of Defense for Italy will seize control of the Italian government. And in England, Sir William MacDonald, current Secretary for Education, will become Prime Minister. The outlier in the group seems to be Vadym Peliura who is a Cabinet Minister in the Ukraine."

"Holy hell!" Buster exclaimed. "Does it say when this is all supposed to happen?"

"Not that I can tell." Quint quickly scanned the rest of the page. "This is not good. It seems that they plan to assassinate President Northrup before the next election. I don't see a specific date. It just says they will do it while he is out of the country, and they will blame it on the Russians. Peliura and Blum are to arrange it when Henderson gives the signal.

"Freddy, I need you to get the original so I can get it to Milan ASAP. In the meantime, I'll get the President and Gerald Williams on the phone as fast as possible. There is an upcoming NATO conference that Northrup is scheduled to attend. The Secret Service needs to be put on high alert unless the President decides to cancel."

Quint stood, "Buster, I need you and Jimmy to keep an eye out for any trouble. Freddy, you should be okay driving to Milan on your own since no one yet knows we have that file."

"Not a problem. As soon as I get this to the courier, I'll come back. If the Director thinks we need backup here, let me know and I'll bring a couple of assets back with me."

Within five minutes of Freddy's departure, Quint had both the President and Director Williams on a conference call. He quickly read through the names in the AFGU file and the roles they were to assume in a united global government. He then explained the method by which they intended to assume control in order to implement AFGU's tenets.

When he had finished, the President sat in stunned silence for a moment before swearing, "That two-faced son-of-a-bitch. I never did like the bastard and to think I let the party talk me into naming him Vice President. Thanks to you, Quint, I believe it is safe to say, AFGU is not going to have a launch date if I can help it."

"Mr. President," Gerald Williams began, "we need the head of the Secret Service in on this. Also, the leaders in both houses of Congress need to be informed. Since we control the Senate, Marcum should be all over this. Speaker of the House, Holts will come along, too, after I detail what's going on. He might hate your guts, but he can't risk getting blamed for your assassination if he doesn't support me in this. It's possible the Vice President has planted lackies to spy for him."

Northrup interrupted, "Until we can ferret out any leaks, I suggest this be kept in utmost secret."

"I agree. I will call all three and ask them to meet us somewhere we won't need to worry about anyone picking up our conversation."

"Director Williams, do you have any suggestions?"

"We have a safe house in the country just over the Maryland line. Our Secret Service Director, Joe Walls, knows where it is. We can get you, Marcum, and Holts there without a problem. I will have them say they have family obligations and are away from their offices for a few hours."

"Good. I will also be calling the leader of each of the countries mentioned beginning with Great Britain. If possible, we need to draw these characters out in the open so they can all be arrested as traitors. Since AFGU has done nothing so far, this will need to be handled with some ruthless diplomacy."

Quint interrupted, "Mr. President, do we really want this made public?"

"What are you getting at, Quint?"

"It seems to me, that this should all be handled quietly to save international embarrassment. Yes, we need to nail the culprits, but there may be a way to do it without raising worldwide alarm. It is especially tricky for us since the Vice President and a Senator are both complicit."

The President chuckled, "Don't worry, Quint. I've got balls enough to handle this."

"Yes, sir. I know you do."

Northrup said, "Director Williams, devise a plan and get back to me. I'm going to hang up now and call the men here that need to be in the loop. As soon as we have a plan, I will call the government heads in England, France, Germany, Italy, and someone we can trust in the Ukraine and let them know what is going on."

When the President had hung up, Quint explained his idea to Gerald about advertising Owens' death and the man's concerns about his estate. The Director readily agreed to take care of it.

"In the meantime, Quint. Hunker down at the villa until I get back to you with a game plan."

Quint was tired. It had been a long and draining day, and he had only a few hours to get some sleep before he would need to take a turn at guard duty. Lila murmured softly and opened her arms to him when he crawled into bed. Although he had planned to go to sleep immediately, the invitation was too enticing to ignore. Afterwards, he said an unaccustomed prayer of gratitude that she had been restored to him unharmed. Sated, he sank into slumber with Lila spooned against him.

While they were having breakfast the next morning, his phone rang. Glancing at the screen, he excused himself so he could talk to Gerald in private to determine what their next steps would be.

Chapter 21

President Northrup leaned back in his chair in the Oval Office. He smiled with satisfaction. He felt he had arrived at the perfect solution. He had talked with the heads of state for England, France, Italy, Germany, and the Ukraine, and all had agreed to his plan. The only remaining detail was to stop the man that had been assigned to assassinate him. He leaned forward and punched in the number for the CIA.

When he had Director Williams on the line, he outlined his proposal before continuing, "I have contacted the concerned countries, and they have all agreed to cooperate. The big issue hanging out there is stopping whoever has been assigned to kill me so Henderson can step into the Presidency. With the very survival of this country at stake, there is no way we can allow that to happen.

"No, sir. I have some ideas. But first I need to know what you have put in place with the leaders of the other countries."

The POTUS detailed his discussion with the other leaders and his solution for the two traitors in the US. In the States, Gerald would be responsible for getting both Henderson and Ogden to Washington.

Gerald readily agreed, "I can handle that. The issue that remains is what we do about your time in Brussels when you will be vulnerable to attack from some really bad actors."

"I will be staying at the Ambassador's residence, Truman Hall. That's secure and will be crawling with security. The only time that I will be more exposed, other than on route from the airport to the residence and then from there to the NATO building, is when I speak to the gathering of twenty-seven members. The press will be in attendance along with various invited guests. I want every single one of them thoroughly vetted. I need you to work with Joe Wall so the Secret Service is informed of schedule details and locations so he can coordinate with the team of Secret Service agents that will be traveling with me. I want both Quint and Buster there. Oh, yes…Mrs. Cord, too. If it were not for those three, we would know nothing about this scheme. Besides, if there is any attempt on my life, I want Quint and Buster to have my back."

"I'll call them and have them fly to Brussels. We need them there ahead of you to get the lay of the land."

Northrup added, "We also need to notify the Ambassador to NATO, Evelyn Kincade, what's up. I think you've met her. Eve needs to be informed that not only my Secret Service detail, but Quint and the other two will be staying in Truman Hall with me. I also want them at the airport when I arrive."

"Yes, I met Evelyn Kincade at a reception in Washington when she was appointed Ambassador. We had a long talk. Knowing her deep sense of patriotism, she will do anything she can to cooperate. Do I need to inform Eve, or will you?"

"Take care of it for me."

"No problem, Mr. President."

"I know I have a top-notch Secret Service, but I don't plan to bring them all in the to-know loop, other than Wall, for fear it will get back to Henderson and screw things up."

"Is there some reason for that, sir?"

"Joe Wall says he can vouch for most of his men, but one of them came over from assignment with Henderson. The man may be totally on the up and up, but we can't risk him leaking to the Vice President about our operation. I want both Ogden and Henderson totally in the dark about why you want them in the Oval Office during my speech."

"Maybe, we should arrange for something that will keep that agent you are worried about on this side of the pond?" Gerald posited.

"Good, that will be one less thing to worry about."

Gerald assured Northrup, "I'll get with Wall and see what we can devise. Trust me: that guy will not be on the NATO team."

"Make sure Ambassador Kincade arranges for full televised coverage of my NATO speech."

"I'll ask her to arrange that when I call. I suspect it will be aired anyway on the evening news.

Northrup emphasized, "It needs to be a live feed from beginning to end. That's critical to my plan."

"I'll make sure of it."

"Great. I'll leave you to it."

* * * * *

The Presidential party spent the night in Truman Hall, the traditional Flemish mansion built for the chocolatier Jean Michiels in 1963, and later donated by his widow to the United States in repayment for saving her country in World War II. The mansion was surrounded by twenty-seven acres of exquisitely landscaped gardens with various guest houses and outbuildings. After a restless night, they all met in the foyer at eight in the morning for the drive to the NATO compound in a Brussels suburb. Of them all, the POTUS appeared the most relaxed and yet he had the most to lose.

President Northrup rode with Ambassador Kincade in the heavily reinforced Presidential limo. Lila, Quint, and Buster were in the next vehicle in the cavalcade, an SUV built like a tank, as were the other vehicles bearing the rest of the security detail. As they drove into the discharge area of NATO headquarters, the three of them admired the large modern steel and glass structure. It was a momentary distraction from worry over what was to come. The POTUS had briefed the Ambassador and the three of them on his plan that depended on several extraneous elements that had to be executed with split second timing in six different countries. The unknown factor was the assassination plan.

After some discussion of their roles in bringing the AFGU scheme to light, the President agreed not to mention Quint, Lila, or Buster by name nor to point them out in his delegation for fear it would compromise future assignments and put a target on their backs.

When he reluctantly agreed to the requested anonymity, the President commented, "It's a shame the world cannot know what the three of you have done to save our country and others from the disastrous destiny this malign group is planning. I assure you I will not forget, and you will be rewarded to the best of my ability."

"Seeing the end of AFGU is reward enough, Mr. President." Quint replied. Lila and Buster both voiced their agreement. After the news article about Lila cracking the previous case, the result of that acclaim had led to her kidnapping. None of them wanted to face another prospect of that ilk.

The three of them exited the heavily reinforced black SUV to stand at attention with the security detail while the President and the Ambassador exited the Presidential limo. It was agreed they would merge with the security detail to keep from drawing attention to their presence. Had it been up to them, they would have been happy to be on a plane on their way home, but the President insisted they stay to watch.

He told them, "I feel safer with you nearby. I want you to keep your eyes peeled in case the assassin was able to slip through our security. Do you have the press passes the Ambassador arranged?"

All three pulled out the plastic nametags dangling from a red cord around their necks that identified them as reporters with the New York Times.

After exiting the limo, Northrup and Kincade walked the red carpet to where Jens Stoltenberg, the Secretary General of NATO stood waiting. Stoltenberg shook hands with Northrup and then Evelyn Kincade before the three turned for the press to take photos. Buster, Quint, and Lila stood behind the security detail in order to be well out of camera range. With the official welcome done, the entire entourage followed Stoltenberg into the starkly modern auditorium where most of the other members of the twenty-seven nation body, as well as various other dignitaries, were already seated in anticipation of Northrup's speech.

On the right side of the stage a video and light control room was partially obscured by a dark glass window. Above that a balcony provided room for security and the press to monitor the auditorium below. Flashing their newly issued press passes, Lila and Quint were directed to the balcony where they mingled with other members of the press. Buster joined the two security men posted off-stage on the left-hand side. Like Quint and Lila, Buster and the security detail all wore Kevlar vests. Each man carried their Glocks in neatly concealed shoulder holsters, and all wore earphones. Buster found a place to stand where he could cover the stage, the balcony, and the right portion of the audience. One of the security guys stood with him while two others stationed themselves on the right side of the stage. When they were in place, Stoltenberg walked to the podium and waited for the lights to dim and the spotlight to illuminate him. After Stoltenberg's introduction, it was the President's turn to stand in the spotlight and give his speech.

The first part of the speech was twenty minutes. During that time, he presented the prepared speech on international trade. In the balcony, Quint and Lila barely heard his words as they mingled among the members of the press. One man stood out. Unlike the others, he was perspiring profusely. Rather than taking notes or talking into a cell phone, he stood near the cameramen. He constantly fiddled with the camera bag hanging from his shoulder. They watched as he glanced around and then loosened the flap on the bag.

Quint murmured in Lila's ear, "I'm signaling Buster to be ready to move. I don't like the looks of that character over there. You see the one?"

"Dark greasy hair, blue sportscoat, no tie, gray slacks?"

"Yeah. My gut tells me he's up to something. I'm going to edge over there by him just in case…"

"Be careful," Lila whispered.

Quint quietly spoke in his earphone. One of the security guys, who had followed them to the balcony, walked over to join him. Together they edged in behind the dark-haired man and waited.

At that moment, Northrup arrived at the critical junction of his speech. Laying his notes aside, he began speaking extemporaneously without using the teleprompter that he had employed for the prepared presentation. Behind him live television feeds from five countries popped up on the blue background of the stage. The audience stirred and murmured among themselves as the President paused. This was not part of the expected agenda, and they all sat confused by the abrupt shift.

At that moment, the dark-haired man on the balcony reached in the camera case that hung from his shoulder and started to extract a gun. Before he could take aim, both Quint and the security detail bull-rushed him to the floor. Quint helped security cuff the man before he faded into the crowd of press who were rushing to photograph the captured man. Signaling to Lila, the two of them left the press area and walked down the stairs where they stood and watched as the President resumed speaking after a glance towards the commotion in the balcony.

Taking a deep breath, President Northrup began, "I recently became aware of a dangerous group of men that have united in a cabal to destroy the very foundations of our countries under the acronym AFGU. The letters stand for the Alliance for Global Unity that goes far beyond the objectives of the United Nations. I will read you their basic tenets, and you will immediately comprehend the immense danger such a group poses for the entire world."

Northrup then detailed the various objectives as, behind him, the leaders of the UK, France, Italy, Germany, and the Ukraine filled the five real-time television screens dedicated to their respective countries. Northrup paused dramatically as each of the leaders watched a handcuffed man being led in and surrounded by guards. After he had introduced the five leaders, he detailed the current positions of the arrested men in the respective countries. He began with the UK.

"The Prime Minister ordered the arrest this morning of Sir William McDonald, Secretary of State for Education, and a founding member of AFGU. On the next screen, you will recognize the President of France with his Ministry of Labor Director, Georges Blum. Direct your attention now to the President of Italy who this morning apprehended Marco Bonafede, his Minister of Defense. The Chancellor of Germany ordered the arrest of Peter Lambrecht, her Minister of Foreign Affairs. Each of these men will now face the justice of their nation's courts.

"Next is Vadym Petliura, a Minister in the government of Ukraine. He was assigned to see that I am assassinated during my time here. Hopefully, I will be able to elude that intended fate. He, too, along with his cohorts will face the wrath of his country.

"That now brings me to the saddest members of all for me and my own country, The United States of America. Two of the men behind AFGU are our citizens and prominent politicians in our government."

The audience gasped as the five screens went blank and one large screen appeared behind the President. Most of them recognized Vice President Henderson sitting on the sofa in the Oval Office. Many recognized Senator Ogden of California and a few could name the man sitting beside them, Gerald Williams, Director of the CIA. They were surrounded by security guards. President Northrup turned to the screen and waited for a moment before he resumed speaking.

"Before you, many will recognize the Vice President of the U.S.A. and Senator Ogden of California. They are being arrested as I speak for their roles in this travesty." The President stopped as every eye swiveled to the gaping mouth of the Vice President whose shock and fear were evident. Ogden began to rise from his seat before he was firmly held in place by one of the guards. Continuing, Northrup said, "It is particularly grievous when members of my own government become traitors to our country, as I am sure it is for the five other leaders you have seen on screen this morning. No doubt many of you were wondering why these five leaders were noticeably absent. Now you know the reason.

"While I cannot name the brave men and woman that made this a failed attempt at world domination, I am sure you will join me in a round of applause for what they have done for us all."

Lila and Quint beamed at one another as the sound of a standing ovation rang in their ears.

Title: *Run Cissy Run*
- Betty J. vaughn
- Language: English
- Hard Cover Book ISBN: 9781590956748
- Paper Back Book ISBN: 9781590956755
- eBook / ePub: ISBN: 9781590956762

Book One

You would think Cecilia LaRoque has it all: a loving father, wealth, beauty, social position and a devoted suitor. She doesn't. Crushed by a cold and critical mother who soon absconds to live with a dissolute lover, 'Cissy' struggles to prove herself worthy of love and respect. She could not have foreseen in her teenage years that the genteel and privileged life she had led would come to a crashing halt with the outbreak of Civil War, a bitter struggle that would tear her world apart. Despite the hardships and inherent danger, she seizes the opportunity to forge an unorthodox role for herself as a spy.

Reviews for *Run Cissy Run*

"*Run, Cissy, Run* is a great book. Trust me, you will not want to put it down."

--Ann Compton

"Just finished reading *Run, Cissy, Run*! Enjoyed it very much!"

--Edie H. Bailey

"I just finished reading *Run, Cissy, Run* and enjoyed it a lot. I like that there is southern history as well as the story, as a lot of it I do not know."

--Sharon E. Brumbaugh

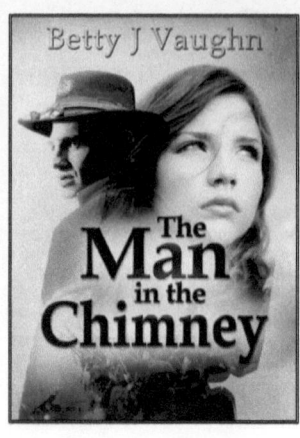

Title: *The Man In The Chimney*
- Betty J. vaughn
- Language: English
- Hard Cover Book ISBN: 9781590956021
- Paper Back Book ISBN: 9781590956038
- eBook / ePub: ISBN: 9781590956045

Book Two

The War Between the States has come to eastern North Carolina, bringing hardships, pillaging, and fear to the local residents. For those left at home, the struggle to procure the needs of daily life is all-consuming; for those serving in the armies of both North and South, death is a daily companion. Against this backdrop, an unlikely and forbidden love affair between a local woman and a Union officer leads to difficult choices for them both—choices that will tear them apart and force them to deal with the abandonment of their dream of a life together.

Despite broken hearts, misunderstandings, and missed chances, Penny and Ryan strive to survive the dangers and ravages of war and make the best of their separate futures. With the surrender of the South at Appomattox, Penny realizes she has one last chance to either find the man she loves or settle for a life alone.

Reviews for *The Man In The Chimney*

"I read *The Man in the Chimney* and loved it. What a beautiful romance Penny and Ryan enjoyed! I look forward to reading the next in the series."

--*Elaine Werner*

"I read *The Man in the Chimney* and *Turbulent Waters*. My favorite part was the author's descriptions of the things the people lived through and how they coped."

--*Leesa Payne*

"The *Man in the Chimney* was fabulous. I could not put it down."

--*Cyndi McNeill*

Title: *Turbulent Waters*
- Betty J. vaughn
- Language: English
- Hard Cover Book ISBN: 9781590951743
- Paper Back Book ISBN: 9781590951750
- eBook / ePub: ISBN: 9781590951767

Book Three

LOVE IS PERSONAL, WAR IS NOT, especially in North Carolina, 1865-1867, during the reconstruction. With a love they are certain will transcend all else, southern belle Penny Kennedy marries Union Officer and attorney, Ryan Madison, despite the condemnation of those around them. The initial days of wedded bliss end abruptly when Marcus, the man who courted Penny for years in anticipation that she would marry him, is arrested for murder, and Ryan is assigned to prosecute him. As hard as this development is to tolerate for Penny, she will discover worse things await her before Ryan and she can attain the life they desire.

Reviews for *Turbulent Waters*

"A sigh of relief was enjoyed when the last page of this book had been read as it fulfilled the desire for a prequel to the author's last two award-winning books, covering an area not discussed in the other books and containing data that preceded incidents in the other books, dealing with the Civil War and the Naval campaign. Many times stories of this war don't even touch on the navy's contributions, nor life in the seaport towns that saw more action than we are led to believe.

--Judge: North Carolina Society of Historians - Elizabeth Sherrill

Historical Novel Writing At Its Best!

What a fabulous read! Ms. Vaughn has really done her research for this, and the other two books, in this series! Set in central and northern North Carolina at the beginning of the Civil War, events continue to unfold for Ryan, the Northern office, and Penny, the Southern lady. Just when you believe things have settled down a bit, more conflict arises in their lives!

Turbulent Waters is actually the 3nd book in the 4-book series. The first book, *Run Sissy Run*: than *Man in The Chimney*, introduces us to Penny and her family, and Ryan. Again, it tremendously researched novel of the times and conflicts found in everyday life. When you think you know what will happen, you don't.

"The author's intense research is evident in all of her historical books. But her ability to keep you on the edge of your seat until the very last page is what makes her books truly shine."

--Paulette B. Wright

Title: *The Intrepid Miss LaRoque*
- Betty J. vaughn
- Language: English
- Hard Cover Book ISBN: 9781590957103
- Paper Back Book ISBN: 9781590957110
- eBook / ePub:: ISBN: 9781590957127

Book Four

When Wilmington falls in February of 1865, Cissy LaRoque no longer needs to spy. That will not stop her from finding a new career where she can prove her worth beyond societal expectations of a woman. With the war drawing to an end and Wilmington occupied, she is faced with desperate circumstances. Ryan Madison, a Union officer from the past, and Brandon McLean, a new one, attempt to help her. While attracted to them both, she is aware of family and community hostility toward the enemy and dares not act on the attraction. Her fiancé, Logan who is fighting for the southern cause, does not arouse her ardor like the two Union men. When the Confederacy falls, she convinces her father to allow her to run his shipping office in New Berne while he maintains the main office in Wilmington. There she discovers Ryan has married and Logan has jilted her. Provoked and titillated by a man she cannot have but craves, she puts aside romance and concentrates on business. Despite her father's initial objections, much to his surprise she succeeds far beyond any expectation. Although she is happy in what she has achieved, she is frustrated by what she has lost.

Reviews for *The Intrepid Miss LaRoque*

Excellent book

--James W. Chesnutt

Title: *Yesterday's Magnolia*
- Betty J. vaughn
- Language: English
- Hard Cover Book ISBN: 9781590955543
- Paper Back Book ISBN: 9781590955550
- eBook / ePub: ISBN: 9781590955567

Jo envies Margo and Maurice for their ready charm, looks, wealth, glamour, and exciting lives never realizing that it is she who is envied for a life that contains the things that they themselves long for and have not attained.

"It's a shame to have so damned much and yet so little." An eastern North Carolina farmer's daughter, Margot, streaks like a comet into the life style of the rich and famous. Her beauty and exuberant, zestful personality gain her entrance to boardrooms, the White House, a corporate jet stocked with Cristal champagne and caviar, a villa in Italy, and marriage to one of the world's most powerful men. Maurice, the spurned suitor, seeks friendship and comfort from Margot's sister, Jo, a quiet, bookish art history teacher. Jo envies them both for their ready charm, looks, wealth, glamour, and exciting lives never realizing that it is she who is envied for a life that contains the things that they themselves have not attained. Like the comets they so resemble both Margot and Maurice are consumed by the friction of life, leaving Jo to remember the magic moments they brought to a more conventional path.

Reviews for *Yesterday's Magnolia*

This was the perfect read during my beach vacation!! It is very much a vicarious escape to Europe similar to "A Year in Province" and "Under the Tuscan Sun" but with a bit more sex thrown in.
--*Susan White*

"The author engages her readers to the last page."
--*Carolyn Asaki*

Title: *Tiger's Code*
- Betty J. vaughn
- Language: English
- Hard Cover Book ISBN: 9781590953907
- Paper Back Book ISBN: 9781590953914
- eBook / ePub: ISBN: 9781590953921

Book One

Quint Cord's latest CIA assignment is proving to be his most challenging and could well lead to catastrophic events if he does not break the code in time to avert them.

Quint Cord is an unlikely spy. With sufficient family money so that he never needs to work, he could have spent his life idling on a beach chasing women. But from the moment he discovers famous codes of the past in a university class, he is hooked. His unique talent for creating and breaking codes brings him to the attention of the CIA.

A powerful and ambitious politician, who's in cahoots with a Saudi prince, plans to seize the US presidency and throw the western world into turmoil. Quint flees the country only to stay one step ahead of a foe determined to kill him before he can break the code.

Clue by clue, Quint begins to zero in on his target but can he stop him in time?

Reviews for *Tiger's Code*

"What a terrific read! The characters are full, and the pace is gripping. I have been a huge fan of Vince Flynn and Tiger's Code is right up there with believable political greed and national security threats that are entirely contemporary. I can't wait to read the next volume in the Quint Cord series."

--*D. L. Soderburg*

"Just finished Tiger's Code: the author moves from historical novels to action packed drama with great skill!!! Really enjoyed the fast-moving pace."

--*April S. Blizzard*

"Tiger's Code was a fabulous book. I look forward to reading your newest book in the series."

--*Sherry P. Riley*

"Tiger's Code is the first book of fiction I've read in decades. The book is exceptionally well done and kept me interested throughout. I am very impressed with the significant amount of research done to make the information in the book realistic. A great movie could be made from this book's story line. I am buying the next one."

--*Thomas Smith*

Title: *Dragon's Sword*
- Betty J. vaughn
- Language: English
- Hard Cover Book ISBN: 9781590953808
- Paper Back Book ISBN: 9781590953815
- eBook / ePub: ISBN: 9781590953822

Book Two

    Quint Cord returns to the CIA when his fiancée is almost killed by an egomaniacal hacker who is determined to use his GPS satellite implanted virus to gain control of governments and transportation networks around the globe. Aided by a North Korean dissident who vows to bring down the Kim Jong Un regime, the hacker uses the North Korean's information to crash ships and missiles in Korea and Japan. The hacker next turns to his own country of China to create friction with the United States. When the North Korean becomes frightened for his life and defects, the hacker flees China for fear he will be exposed. Lila Carson, Quint's fiancée, is again on the trail of the hacker as he goes dark to elude discovery.

    From North Carolina to Japan and China, and then to Seattle, Quint struggles to capture the man before he can commit more murder and chaos.

Reviews for Dragon's Sword

"The book is a quick read because it is so interesting. The author has a real talent for capturing the reader's attention and sustaining that momentum throughout the course of the book."
--Dr. Judith Conway Gordon, Retired English Professor

"I loved Dragon's Sword!! Great action and pace. I didn't want it to end, but alas, it did and now I look forward to the next Quint Cord book."
--D. L. Soderburg

"Dragon's Sword is a good read. Informative and yet fast paced."
--Clay Brumbaugh

"Loved Dragon's Sword and couldn't put it down."
--Lou Cunningham

"Dragon's Sword was so good. Totally going to get the next one in the series."
--Kathy M. Jobe

"Another GREAT book! I just finished Dragon's Sword---couldn't put it down. I enjoyed the suspense and intrigue and can only imagine it may seem only too real to our intelligence community. Well done! I look forward to the next book in the Quint Cord series."
--Elizabeth Atwater

Title: *Lyon's Claw*
- Betty J. vaughn
- Language: English
- Hard Cover Book ISBN: 9791590958000
- Paper Back Book ISBN: 9781590955598
- eBook / ePub: ISBN: 9781590955604

Book Three

Lila and Quint Cord are honeymooning in the south of France when Lila is kidnapped. Seized because of her hacking expertise, her captor plans to use her in a deadly game of revenge. While Quint and three CIA operatives work to free her, another and more dangerous plot unfolds with global implications. With hired assassins on their heels, Quint and the other agents must discover what secrets led to the enmity between Lila's captor and his nemesis, recover Lila, and stop the realization of a deadly plot.

Reviews for *Lyon's Claw*

"Great Books! You write one suspenseful thriller right after another. It is difficult for an author to capture my attention to the extent that I do not want to stop reading, but you have succeeded in doing that. The Quint Cord book series would make wonderful movies that would keep the audience on the edge of their seats."

--*Dr. Judith Gordon*

"This gifted author of eight books is adept at writing nail-biting thrillers that sustain excitement and reader interest from cover to cover."

--*Joanna Meredith*

"Another GREAT book! I just finished Dragon's Sword---couldn't put it down. I enjoyed the suspense and intrigue and can only imagine it may seem only too real to our intelligence community. Well done! I look forward to the next book in the Quint Cord series Lyon's Claw."

--*Elizabeth Atwater*